Something

Something

All the Things: part one

K. A. LAST

www.kalastbooks.com.au

K. A. Last
kalast@kalastbooks.com.au
www.kalastbooks.com.au

ISBN: 978-0-6480257-3-3

Formatting and cover design by KILA Designs
www.kiladesigns.com.au
Cover images: ©bigstockphoto.com

Editing by Lauren Clarke Editing
www.laurenclarkeediting.com

For my sixteen-year-old self.
If only I knew then what I know now.

Contents

The damage is already done

The words on the page in front of me blur, and I drop my pen onto my desk. It rolls off and lands on the carpet beside my foot. With a sigh, I swivel in my chair. I stare at the pen for a moment before bending to pick it up.

Study is the last thing I want to be doing on a Saturday night, but term three starts on Monday and trial HSC exams are in two weeks. I worked hard to earn my scholarship, and I don't want to disappoint Mum and Dad. They have big dreams of me becoming a lawyer or a doctor. I have to keep my grades up.

I roll the pen between my fingers and turn back to my history text, blinking a few times. Outside, a car door slams and a voice yells something, but I don't catch the words. I glance up at the clock. It's almost eleven-thirty pm. No wonder my eyes are blurry.

Usually when I hear a car outside I go to the window to see if it's Levi White. But tonight, I need to get through thirty more pages on Egypt and the pyramids.

Something crashes. I jump.

I put my pen down and go to my window anyway, glancing out to our front yard below.

Next door, the veranda light shines brightly into the darkness. Levi sits on the wooden boards, his feet hanging over the top step, staring at a pot plant lying broken on his front path.

I bite my lip. Levi's mum, Yvonne, is not going to be happy.

The front door opens, and Levi's mum comes out, pulling her dressing gown tight around herself. She says something to him, but I can't make out the words.

I unlatch the lock on my window and slide the bottom sash up.

Yvonne speaks again, and this time I hear her. "Did you drive home?"

Levi's car is in the driveway, but it wasn't there half an hour ago. I'd checked.

"No, Mum ... Jarred ..." Levi trails off. He's still sitting on the veranda, his upper body swaying from side to side.

"He better not have been drinking. You know—"

"He wasn't," Levi says. "I'm not stupid, Mum."

Yvonne glances up at my window. *Shit!* My heart beats faster. I dart backwards.

I don't want her to know I'm watching them. I'm pretty sure she doesn't want me to ogle her son and the mess he's made. Or hear their conversation about drink driving.

If Levi has been drinking, how can he do this to her?

Something

His brother only died a year ago, killed in a car accident when he got behind the wheel drunk.

I miss him.

He was like an older brother to me, sometimes better than my own.

Mason would never have turned his back on me like his brother has. Ever since I landed that scholarship, Levi has been different. On my first day at his preppy private school, he pretended not to know who I was. It's like I'm his dirty little secret that no one can ever discover.

I move back to the window and pull the curtains closed, leaving a small gap in the middle so I can see what's happening.

Levi gets to his feet and turns away from his mum. His foot slips, and he tumbles down the stairs. He lands in the mess of the pot plant, sprawling onto the path and face-planting the concrete. I wince.

Yvonne shakes her head and swipes at her cheek. She makes her way down the steps to Levi, her mouth moving in a low whisper. She crouches and tries to help him up, but he shoves her hands away.

"You're bleeding," she says. "Come inside."

"Leave me alone!" Levi shouts.

I suck in a sharp breath and hold it, glancing around, expecting someone in our quiet street to react to Levi's loud yell. But most of the houses are dark. They stay that way, and no one comes outside.

Levi glares at his mum. Blood runs from a cut on his cheekbone.

Yvonne stands. "I'll leave the door unlocked," she says before going inside.

3

I grip the edge of the curtains and stare down at Levi. What's happened to him? His gaze flicks towards me, and I quickly step back, my heart racing again.

I stand in the middle of my room and twist my fingers together. I shouldn't be spying on him. He's drunk and injured, so I should help him, but he didn't want his mum's assistance, so why would I be any different? Besides, it's not like he's been nice to me the past couple of years.

A car door slams, and when I go back to the window, Levi is sitting on the lawn with his knees up and his head hanging between them. His fingers grip the neck of a bottle of bourbon. He raises his head and stares at my window, then brings the bottle to his lips and takes a swig. I should step back again, but I can't. My gaze is glued to Levi's face.

The pain in his eyes sears its way through my heart.

What happened to the boy I have loved my entire life?

How did he become so broken?

He shakes his head and looks away, then flops back onto the grass.

I want to go and see if he's okay.

But I don't.

I back away from the window and sit at my desk, my history book open where I left off. I try to concentrate on studying, but ten minutes pass and my thoughts keep returning to Levi. I can't stop glancing at the window and wondering if I should go downstairs and see if he's okay.

"Katie, are you still studying?" Mum's voice makes me jump, and I drop my pen on the desk.

"You scared me," I say.

"Everything all right?" She leans against my open

door and crosses her arms.

I shrug. "Levi's out on the lawn. He's drunk."

Mum frowns. "I heard the yelling." She goes to my window and peeks through the gap in the curtains. "Maybe you should go and see if he's okay."

"It's late, Mum."

"Yeah, but it's Saturday night." She glances at my clock and smiles. "Tomorrow is the last day of the holidays, and you have a bit over an hour before curfew."

"He's a big boy, Mum. I'm sure he'll be fine." I tap my pen on my desk.

Mum sighs. "He might need a friend to talk to, Katie. See you in the morning." She pulls my door closed, and I listen to her pad down the hallway to her bedroom.

I take my glasses off and rub my eyes. Maybe Levi does need a friend, but that *friend* isn't me. With a deep breath, I push my glasses back up my nose and return to the window, pulling the curtains aside.

Levi hasn't moved from his position on the lawn. His gaze locks with mine as if he's been expecting me to come back. He gets to his feet and staggers a couple of steps to his veranda, avoiding the smashed flower pot. I raise my hand and give him a half-hearted wave and a close-lipped smile. He scoffs and shakes his head, and I regret even looking at him. He puts a foot on the first step and clutches the railing.

I turn away from the window, go to my desk, and close my text book. I think I'm done for tonight. Levi's reaction has gotten under my skin, but I told myself a long time ago that there are worse things in life than people laughing at me.

My eyes are heavy, so I take my glasses off and set them on my desk. I flick my overhead light off and get changed into my PJs by the light of the reading lamp attached to my bedhead. The covers are cool when I slip between them. I lie back and stare at my ceiling, counting the stars my brother, Daniel, and I stuck up there when we were kids. They've been there so long they don't glow much anymore. I want them to glow again. Maybe I'll replace them.

I reach up to turn off the lamp when something taps on my window. The curtains move, and Levi sticks his head through the open section at the bottom, a frown on his face. I scramble to sit up and grab my glasses, putting them on.

Oh God, I'm in my PJs. I grip the edge of the covers and pull them up to my chest.

"What the hell are you doing?" I ask in a whisper.

He mutters something I can't make out, then he tumbles through and lands in a heap on the window seat before falling to the floor. My journal lands beside him with a thud.

Levi pushes himself up and sits with his back resting against the wall. His head lolls onto the seat cushion.

I have no words.

Levi White just climbed in my window.

He hasn't done that since the middle of tenth grade, when he found out about my scholarship.

Levi raises his head and studies me. "Stop opening and closing your mouth, Katie. You look like a fish."

I finally find my voice. "I ... what ... how did you not fall and kill yourself?"

He gets to his feet then plonks down on the end of my bed, almost falling off.

"I haven't forgotten how to climb—"

"What do you want?" I keep my voice low.

"You waved. I came." He smiles.

"I was trying to offer you a little support," I say. "Not asking you to scale the side of my house and fall through my window."

"Your trellis is still pretty sturdy ... even after all this time."

I scoff. "I remember the last time you climbed it." My heart lurches at the memory.

"So do I," he says.

Levi's eyelids are droopy, and he closes his eyes for a second. I take the opportunity to stare at his face. Despite how he's treated me, he's still the boy next door who I fell in love with in kindergarten. And I'm secretly glad he's climbed into my room. *Maybe ...*

I shake my head, refusing to entertain something that's impossible.

"That looks nasty." I point to the bloody cut on his left cheek.

"It didn't tickle," Levi says. "My hand hurts, too." He frowns and looks down to where his right hand rests on his leg.

"Wait here." I throw the covers aside and go to my door.

Levi smiles a lopsided, drunken smile. "Nice PJs."

I roll my eyes and inch the door open, escaping into the hallway, thankful Levi can't see me blush. Having him see me in baby pink flannel pants covered with little white sheep is embarrassing.

Dad's soft snores float down the hallway. Daniel is out, but I check the hall anyway, then go to the bathroom to grab a wet face washer and some Dettol.

Back in my room, Levi is lying on his side on my bed with his head propped up on his elbow.

"Are you going to tend to my wounds?" His smile widens.

Levi is muscular and gorgeous, and I want to do more than tend his wounds, but I'm not about to tell him that—especially while he's being an idiot.

"Don't be a jerk." I perch on the edge of the bed, pouring some Dettol onto the face washer. "Sit up."

Levi shuffles behind me and drops his legs over the side of the mattress, moving until he's beside me. I dab his cheek with the wet cloth.

"Ouch!" Levi's smile falls away, and he winces.

"You really should ice it ... to stop any swelling."

Levi grabs my hand and pulls it gently away from his face. "Why are you so nice to me?"

"I *try* to be nice to everyone."

"You shouldn't."

I stare at his hand holding mine, and I want him to be holding me in other ways, but it's never going to happen. Outside this room we can't be friends. Not anymore.

"What's the point in being mean to people?" I say. "It only makes you unhappy."

"Some people deserve it."

"That's true."

Levi's grip on my wrist tightens. "Katie ..."

I stare into his deep brown eyes. "Levi." I hold my breath.

Something

He tears his gaze away from mine and looks at his fingers wrapped around my wrist. "Don't tell anyone about this." He lets go, and my skin is cold where he's been touching me.

"Don't tell anyone about your drunken fall down your front steps, or don't tell anyone you climbed in my window?"

"Both," he says.

I lick my lips and chew on the bottom one. "Who would I tell?"

I take his injured hand and look at his palm. There are some cuts on it, so I swab them with Dettol as well. He winces again.

"Don't be such a baby," I say, but I stop anyway.

We sit in silence. I fold the face washer and rest it on the edge of my desk.

"Your mum seemed upset," I say to try and break the tension in the air.

"She's always upset."

"Why? Because of … Mason?"

Levi scoots around me and flops back onto my pillow. "I'm not having this conversation with you. I don't want to talk about it."

"Then why are you here?" I ask. Right now, I'm not sure if I'm mad because he won't talk to me, or happy because he climbed in my window in the first place.

"I have no idea, Katie." He rolls his head to the side and closes his eyes.

"Well, it couldn't be because we're friends, now, could it?"

Levi opens his eyes but doesn't move. I blink a few times then look away, pushing my glasses up my nose.

9

"I miss you," Levi says. The words were whispered, but they were there.

I want to tell him I miss him, too. But do I really want to open old wounds?

I press my lips together. "Why are you drowning your sorrows in a bottle of bourbon?" I ask instead. "Drinking isn't the answer to anything, Levi. You, of all people—"

"Should know that? Yeah. I should. But you don't ..." He puts a hand over his face and lets out a long breath. "You have no idea."

There are a lot of things I could say to him, like *alcohol makes it worse*, or *you're not the only one with problems*. But how could I say anything like that when I really don't know what he's going through right now? As much as I loved Mason like a brother, I've never lost a real family member.

Besides, I have my own problems without having to worry about Levi's. He's the type of guy who's had everything handed to him. I have to work for everything I get, and being considered trash in a private school is pretty lonely. Mr Popularity, Levi White, is the last person who would ever understand loneliness.

Levi picks up one of the stuffed teddies on my bed and stares at it for a minute before handing it to me. I hug it to my chest. He sits, and shuffles back against the bedhead.

"You still like that kind of shit?" he asks.

I stare at the white bunny in my hands. It has big floppy ears and a pink tummy, and it's my favourite. I nod but don't say anything, putting it back with the others and going to sit at my desk.

Something

Levi scoots to the edge of the bed and clumsily puts his feet on the floor. He grabs the book from my desk.

"History," he says.

"You should be studying, too." I pick up my pen and glance at my clock. It's well past midnight.

He laughs and puts the book back, then rubs his temples. "Study isn't really my thing."

"What is?" I put my pen down and swivel my chair to face him. I may have known Levi my whole life, and we may have been best friends once, but now, I don't *really* know him anymore.

Levi shrugs. "I don't know what I want to be when I grow up." He grins.

I ignore his stupid comment. "What are you good at? There must be something, other than everyone loving you."

Levi runs a hand through his mess of dark brown hair. I want to reach out and run my fingers through it, too. The thought makes me almost laugh out loud, and a blush heats my cheeks. As if I would ever be the one who got to do something like that.

"I don't know. Maybe … science. Or marine biology." He goes quiet and stares at his hands. "It's stupid. I'm not smart enough."

"I could help you study … if you like." I hold my breath, hoping he'll say yes because it will be an excuse to spend time with him.

"I probably won't remember this conversation tomorrow." Levi looks up.

I scoff, and suddenly, I'm mad. As if we could ever be friends again. It's obvious he's looking for an out. Well, if

that's what he wants, I'll give it to him. "If you *really* want help with your homework, you'll remember. The window's that way." I point, before swivelling to face my desk.

"Do you want me to leave?"

"That would be good." I stare at my closed history book.

"Are you angry with me?"

I look up. "No, Levi. I'm not angry with you. Being angry is something a *friend* would do when their other friend behaved like an arse."

"You think I'm an arse?"

"Yes ... a drunk one."

"Why?"

"Gee, I don't know." I stand and my chair spins. "Maybe because this is the first time we've had a real conversation in two years, and you want me to not tell anyone. And I get it. You're the popular rich guy, and I'm the scholarship girl who's poor and worth shit. You don't want to be associated with me."

"That's not true."

"The hell it isn't," I say. "Your parents should've moved you all to one of the ritzy suburbs instead of rebuilding here. Then you could hang out with the rich people twenty-four-seven."

"I like it here." He frowns.

"Yeah, well, since my first day in year eleven when you pretended you didn't know me, nothing has changed."

Levi rolls off the bed and sways towards me. "I am an arse."

"A drunk one."

"I'm sorry ... I'll go."

Something

I shake my head, and cross my arms in an attempt to seem pissed off when really, all I am is sad. He probably *won't* remember anything in the morning, and we'll go back to being neighbours who used to be best friends but now never speak to each other.

"Don't break your neck on the way down," I say.

He climbs onto the window seat and puts one leg through the open window, then pauses on the sill. "Do you want to know why I came up here?"

"I get the feeling you're going to tell me anyway."

"Of all the people I know, Katie, you always look for something good in everyone, even the people who hurt you. Maybe ... maybe I need someone to see the good in me. And maybe I don't want to hurt you anymore." He turns and is out the window and on the trellis before I have time to think of a reply.

I watch him cross the grass and then step through the garden bed on our boundary. When he reaches the veranda, he glances back, and I move away from the window so he can't see my wet cheeks.

"It's too late, Levi," I whisper to the open window.

The damage is already done.

2

You never know unless you try

I don't see Levi again for the rest of the weekend. His car isn't in the driveway all day Sunday. I try to study for our upcoming exams, but I can't concentrate, so I resort to quality time with my iPod and my journal.

I don't write in it as much as I used to. These days I can't find many things I want to remember. Levi climbing in my window is the first note-worthy event that's happened in a while. My biggest thought is *how can he come up here and pretend like nothing happened, after all this time?*

Now, I'm standing on the corner waiting for the bus. Levi's BMW is parked on the street. It takes me a bus ride, a train trip, and a ten-minute walk to reach the back gates of school, a total of around forty-five minutes. Levi can drive it in twenty, but he's never offered me a lift.

"Hey, Katie." Jessica Hart from a few houses down the

street stops beside me, her school folder clutched to her chest. "Ready for first day back?"

"Not even," I say. "You?"

She shrugs. "I guess."

We stand together, our blue tartan skirts the perfect private-school length, just above the knee. Our white button-up blouses are freshly pressed. We both look the part, only I feel like an imposter.

Jessica and I are good friends, and like me and Levi, we grew up together. The only difference is she didn't ditch me when I started private school.

It's no secret my family is not as well off as some families in the street, but it's never mattered to Jessica. When she found out I would be going to school with her for our final two years, she was over the moon.

A blue Honda Civic passes us and Jessica's twin sister, Josephine, honks the horn, then flips us the bird.

"Charming," I say. "I can't believe she never drives you."

"That's because she's a bitch," Jessica says, so matter-of-factly that I laugh.

"I don't think I can disagree."

Jessica shrugs. "It's cool. She spent her eighteenth birthday money on a car. I'm saving mine for an overseas trip. And Levi never drives you." Jessica glances at me sideways. She knows how hurt I was when he stopped talking to me.

"That's because he's a jerk, *and* an arse."

Jessica laughs as well.

The bus pulls up to the kerb, and air whooshes as the doors open. We climb on and take our usual seats in the middle.

"You been studying?" Jessica asks.

I smile. "What else would I be doing?"

"You'll get dux. I know you will."

"That's the plan. I've already written my speech … Just in case."

Jessica grins back at me.

When we get to school, Jessica and I go to the office to scan our student cards that record our attendance for the day. The halls buzz with commotion as we make our way to our lockers. The first bell sounds and students dart in every direction. I switch out my English and math books for first and second period, then slam my locker shut.

"Hey," Karen, my best friend, says. "What exciting things did you get up to since I saw you last?" She leans against the lockers and bites into an apple.

"What could've possibly happened between Friday night and now?" I desperately want to tell her about Levi climbing in my window, but I told him I wouldn't say anything, even though he probably doesn't deserve my loyalty. "What do you think I did?"

"Made mad passionate love to Levi while studying." Karen smirks.

I stare at her as if she's grown horns. "You're the devil."

"I think she just did the study part," Jessica says.

"Whoa, speaking of the devil." Karen looks over my shoulder. "What happened to his face?"

I turn and follow her stare. The cut on Levi's cheek looks worse in daylight. It's scabbed over, but the edges of the wound are bruised and purple.

"That looks … sore," I say.

"Ouch," Jessica says, then she sighs. "How is he still

so pretty?"

Karen and I exchange a glance, and she laughs.

Levi saunters along the hall, his hands stuffed in his pockets, surrounded by his pack of loyal followers.

The in-crowd consists of the richest kids in the grade. Karen hates them, and not because they have more money than her, but because most of them aren't very nice people.

I try not to hate anyone, but some people make it pretty hard.

"What are you staring at?" Veronica Porter snaps. She hangs at Levi's side, keeping her distance from me, as if she's afraid she'll catch poor people.

Karen puts her hands on her hips. "The hole in your face that noise comes out of."

"Oh, bitch much?" Veronica's sidekick, Rachel, asks. "She's looking for trouble."

Josephine glares at Jessica but doesn't say anything.

"Did everyone have a great break?" Britney, our vice-captain, asks in her high-pitched voice.

We all ignore her.

"I'm not the one who's the bitch," Karen says.

I cringe and put my hand on her arm. "Don't. Please."

She doesn't listen.

"What happened to your face, Levi?" Karen says as he levels with us. "Veronica have a good chew?"

"Shut it," Veronica says.

Levi's mates, Jarred Lewis and Geoff Wilcox, walk up behind the girls. Levi steps around all of them and glances at me as he passes, but I can't read his expression. I have no idea if he remembers anything he said to me on

Saturday night, and knowing he is so much kinder than any of these rich snobs tears a hole in my heart. I want my Levi back—only I don't know where he's gone.

"No one said you could talk." Jarred gets in Karen's face, but she doesn't back up. She's tougher than I could ever be.

"No one tells me what to do," Karen says.

Jarred narrows his eyes.

"Someone should." Geoff pushes past her.

"Cut it." Levi glances back but doesn't meet my stare, even though I'm glaring at him.

Jarred clenches his jaw then moves away, walking a few steps backwards towards Levi before turning around and falling into step with him and Geoff.

I lock gazes with Veronica, unable to believe she's the girl all the other girls want to be. She steps towards me and rakes my folder and books from my hands. They scatter onto the hallway floor, papers falling from my folder and fluttering everywhere. Her friends laugh.

"Don't forget who you are," Veronica says before catching up to the boys.

Rachel follows, muttering words like 'trash' and 'slut' under her breath.

"I guess it's my job to try and control this situation," Britney says, rolling her eyes. She walks off in a huff.

Josephine is the only one who hesitates. "You shouldn't make her mad." She's looking at Jessica, but I know she's talking to all of us.

"Veronica is such a bitch." Karen kneels and helps me gather my papers and books from the floor.

"Just … be careful," Josephine says before walking away.

Something

Jessica sighs. "I don't know why she's friends with them."

"Because she's a try-hard loser," Karen says.

I frown. "Don't say that about Jess's sister."

"It's true." She hands me my folder. "Jess is so nice. And Josie is just … as much of a bitch as Veronica. How is that even possible? They're identical. It's like Josie's personality got switched at birth or something."

"She's not that bad at home," Jessica says.

"You shouldn't react," I say to Karen. "It only makes it worse. You should know by now that reacting is what they want."

"You should react more," she says. "Stand up for yourself."

"I don't care what they think. I want to get good grades, so I can live my parents' dream, then get out of this hellhole." I stare down the hall after the group that rules the twelfth grade.

"I rest my case." Karen puts a hand on her hip. "You need to live your own dream."

I sigh. "Can we not talk about this now?"

The second bell blares through the sound system, and Karen, Jessica, and I make our way to first-period English. We take our seats in the front row as the rest of the class trickles in. Veronica sashays down the aisle to take her seat in the back, and I have to resist the urge to turn around and glare at her.

Moments later, a screwed up ball of paper hits me in the back of the head. As much as I'm curious to see what derogatory remark Veronica has written to me, I ignore it and take my books from my bag, setting them neatly on my desk.

Levi walks in, his backpack slung casually over his shoulder. He comes to the far aisle where my desk is and turns. I watch him go to the back of the room and take a seat beside Veronica. She smiles smugly, and I face the front of the room again. There's nothing going on between them as far as I know, but even though she's with Jarred I think she'd jump at the chance to be with Levi if she could. Every girl in the school would.

I turn again to glance at Levi. He's sitting back in his chair with his arms folded. He raises his eyebrows at me, and I look away quickly. There was no reason for him to walk down my aisle. He could have easily cut across the room, and the fact he didn't annoys me. What's he trying to prove? Does he want me to pay attention to him? Because if he does, he's going about it the wrong way.

Karen clicks her fingers in front of my face. "Hello ... Earth to Katie."

"Sorry." I blink and give her a tentative smile.

"Where did you go?"

I sigh. "Nowhere you can come."

"I hope it was nice."

Our English teacher, Mrs Wu, finally makes an appearance. She struts in, her skirt billowing around her legs and her glasses bouncing against her chest where they hang from a beaded chain. She puts her folder on her desk and sets her iPad on top. Before she speaks, the class waits as she makes a quick headcount and records it.

"Hello, class," Mrs Wu says. "Welcome to term three. Your trial exams start in exactly two weeks. Today, you will focus on revision. You know the texts we've covered.

Something

I don't mind what you revise, but I don't want any noise, and I don't want anyone out of their seats." The class groans. "Face the front. Books out. No talking." Mrs Wu sits at her desk, puts her glasses on, and opens her folder.

I do as she says and open my copy of *The Great Gatsby*. I figure re-reading it is as good a place to start as any.

Five minutes later, another ball of paper hits me in the back of the head. It bounces off my shoulder and lands on the floor between my foot and the low shelves that line the window side of the classroom. I check Mrs Wu isn't watching before bending down, pretending to get something from my bag, and scooping the paper into my hand. With my hands under the desk I slowly un-crumple the ball then lay it flat on my desk.

I bite my lip as I read the words.

Truth or dare, Katie? V.

Great. Getting sucked into the in-crowd's stupid games is the last thing I need. The whole grade knows they play truth or dare on a regular basis, and if you're one of the less-popular kids, it's not good if they single you out. The only advantage to playing is I would get to go next, but I can't single out Veronica since she's truth-or-dared me.

Whatever she's trying to do, I'm not buying into it. I screw the paper up again and stuff it into the pocket of my uniform. I'm not playing.

For the rest of English class, the words *truth or dare* run over and over in my mind. I'm surprised no one has challenged me before, but I've heard stories about some of the stupid things people have done. I'm not sure what I'd choose if Veronica made me pick one. Or what would scare me most—the question she'd ask or the thing she'd dare me to do.

I have no desire to find out, either way.

"What did it say?" Karen asks as I leave English with her and Jessica.

I pull the note from my pocket and hand it to her without saying anything. She smooths it between her fingers, and Jessica looks over her shoulder.

"Oh no," Jessica says. "This is bad."

"I'm not answering it," I say. "Veronica can get stuffed."

"You have to answer." Jessica's eyes widen. "Or she'll make your life hell. You can't ignore a challenge to truth or dare."

"Veronica already makes my life hell." I raise my eyebrows. "And I can ignore her as much as I like."

"Remember what happened to Karen last year when she tried to ignore it?" Jessica says.

"Yeah, that was fun," Karen says. "Not."

Karen ended up being called in to see the school counsellor because they thought she had a drug problem. Veronica had spread a rumour that Karen was a pothead. She even planted a zip-lock bag in Karen's backpack.

Karen got suspended for three days and had to be interviewed by the police. It took a while for the hype to die down, even though the students knew it was a load of bull. The teachers took a bit more convincing.

"You don't want to get suspended," Jessica says.

"No one is getting suspended," I say. "Veronica can throw whatever she has at me."

"But you're set to be dux. She could ruin it for you."

Karen stops walking and grabs my arm. "This could be the perfect opportunity."

"For what?" I ask.

"To prove to Levi he made a mistake when he dumped you as a friend."

"I don't have to prove anything to anyone." I take the paper from Karen and rip it in half. "I'll see you at lunch."

I stomp off down the hall towards math class, which ends up being more of the same—revision for the upcoming trial exams. Thankfully, Veronica is not in my class, because there's no way I'm answering her note.

I spend most of the lesson thinking about what I said to Karen and Jessica, and I decide my words were true enough. The only person I have anything to prove to is myself.

But what if Jessica is right? What if Veronica decides to ruin my chances at being dux?

I push the thought away and try to focus on the text book in front of me.

At recess, I switch out my English and math books for history and art, then head to the library to renew my copy of *Gatsby*.

On my way to History, I flick through my text book to find where I was up to on Saturday night. My feet twist together. I fall. My history book flies from my grasp, lands on the hallway floor, and skids to the wall. The lockers bang as I grab for something to stop myself, but I cut my palm as it slides over one of the metal hinges. My right knee smacks into the ground before the rest of me follows. The impact knocks my glasses off, and they clatter to the floor.

I don't need to look up to know who tripped me.

Veronica laughs. "Oops. You should watch where you're

going, Katherine."

With my good hand, I push myself to a sitting position then grab my glasses and put them back on. My right palm is bleeding and my knee aches, but I get to my feet as quickly as I can. When I look towards Veronica, Levi and Jarred are there, too. Levi's brow is knitted, and he has his hands stuffed in his pockets. Jarred snickers.

"Karma's a bitch, Veronica," I say. But I'm not looking at her. I'm looking at Levi. How can he let her do this to me?

"Yeah, whatever. And so are you."

"Ronnie. That's enough. Let's go." Levi walks away with Jarred.

Veronica laughs and follows the boys. "You still need to answer me," she calls over her shoulder.

Like hell I do.

Jessica's best friend, Stacey MacDonald, comes over to me, her folder clutched to her chest. "You okay?"

"Yeah, I'll be fine."

Stacey smiles warmly. "Want any help?"

"Really, I'm okay. You'll be late for class. I'll see you at lunch."

I collect my book from the floor and head to the bathroom. The cut on my hand isn't bad, but by the time I clean myself up and get to History, I'm late.

Mr Jenkins glances up from his desk as I enter the room.

"Sorry, sir," I say.

"I don't want to hear your excuse. Take a seat, Katherine. We're concentrating on revision."

Veronica sniggers from the back of the room.

Something

"Is there a problem, Miss Porter?" Mr Jenkins asks.

She puts her head down and doesn't answer. Rachel is sitting beside Veronica. She smirks at me and narrows her eyes. I quickly look away.

Levi isn't in his usual seat, and when I take a quick glance around the room, I can't find him. He must have skipped, which is odd, because he was there when Veronica tripped me.

I slide into my seat in the front row and open my text book to where I was up to. As hard as I try, I can't concentrate, and I can't stop thinking about Levi. He's the school captain. He can't skip classes.

Something must be wrong.

When the bell rings, I jump, and I can't get out of the classroom fast enough.

My knee throbs as I walk to Art. Thankfully, by lunch it's reduced to a dull ache. I find Karen, Jessica, and Stacey on the seats by the oval, already eating. I haven't had anything since breakfast, and I should put something in my stomach, but I've lost my appetite.

"Are you limping?" Karen asks as I sit down.

"It's nothing." I don't want to talk about what happened with Veronica.

"What's up with Levi's face today?" Stacey takes a bite of her sandwich. "What happened to him, Katie?"

"How should I know?" I say a little too defensively.

"Thought you might have heard something." Stacey shrugs. "You're his neighbour."

"That doesn't give me automatic rights to know everything about him," I say.

"It's a pretty big scrape," Karen says.

Stacey chews her food. "Maybe he got into a fight."

"With who?" I ask. "Everybody loves Levi. He'd never fight with his mates."

"I heard his parents fight a lot. Especially after what happened with Mason." Stacey looks at me. "Do they?"

I shake my head. "I don't hear them if they do."

Which isn't the whole truth, but I'm not about to tell them I've heard the odd argument. Everyone argues at some point, and it's none of my business. As far as I know, Levi's parents are great. Even though I haven't had a proper conversation with them in a while, I did grow up half-living in their house. I don't remember anything bad happening. Levi's dad was just, there.

"He probably fell over, drunk or something," Jessica says.

I press my lips together. "What makes you think that?"

"Josie tells me about the parties they go to all the time. He's always a total mess, stumbling all over the place."

I frown but don't say anything.

"Speaking of parties, we should start thinking about what we're going to wear to the formal," Karen says.

"What, now?" I ask. "It's almost two months away. They haven't even announced the theme yet."

"You know the committee likes to keep everyone in suspense," Karen says. "Who cares about the theme? It's a minor detail. We're not going dressed as fish or something. We need to be prepared."

"Fish? You're weird. And I'm hanging on the edge of my seat." I roll my eyes.

"We should try and get the best dresses before they

all disappear," Jessica says.

Stacey nods. "It's our last chance to make a statement."

"About what?" I ask.

"Okay, not a statement. But it's our last chance to get noticed," Karen says. "We can look just as awesome as Veronica and her bitches."

"You're all crazy." I laugh. "There's no way I'm even going."

Karen's mouth drops open. "Of course you're going."

"You have to go," Stacey says.

"We can go together." Jessica looks between each of us. "Has anyone, you know … been asked?"

I laugh. "I think you know what I'm going to say."

"Come on, Katie." Karen grabs my hand and kisses it like I'm a princess and she's the prince. "It will be a splendid night."

Really? My idea of a great night involves a packet of Tim Tams and a good book. Not fancy dresses and uncoordinated dancing.

My friends start talking about dress colours and styles, and I shake my head. I scan the seats around the oval, searching for Levi, but I can't find him in his usual place. Veronica catches me looking in her group's direction and she stands up, putting her hands on her hips.

Karen follows my gaze. "You know you're going to have to play eventually."

"She can't force me to do anything," I say.

"You should just get it over with." Jessica picks at her nails and doesn't look at me. "It's the best way."

"I'm not bowing to her," I say. "She can take her truth or dare and stick it."

Jessica sighs. "It's your funeral." She grabs her bag and gets to her feet. "I'm going to the library."

"I'll come with." Stacey jumps up and the two of them walk together.

Karen studies me. "You're not telling me something."

"I don't know what you're talking about."

"You've been funny all day. You're looking for Levi more than usual. I can tell."

Sometimes I hate that she knows me so well. "Maybe I'm worried about him. I'm allowed to be, aren't I?"

"Why don't you just talk to him, Katie?"

I stare at Karen and raise my eyebrows. "Veronica won't let me within spitting distance. And even if I do talk to him, what would I say?"

Karen shrugs. "You never know unless you try."

My answer is yes

After dinner with Mum and Dad, I head up to my room to study. A light breeze wafts through my open window. I take a moment to peek outside.

Levi's car is in the driveway, and the streetlight reflects off its shiny, black surface. I should ask him what Veronica's problem is, what his problem is, but there's no way I'm going over there.

I sit on the edge of my bed and stare at the books scattered all over it. I'm not sure where to start with study tonight. I'm finding it hard to concentrate again. My knee aches, and my palm is itchy. Since I got home, all I've been able to think about is what happened at school today with Veronica, especially the truth or dare challenge.

A door slams, and I go back to the window. Levi jumps down the front steps of his veranda. The mess from the smashed pot has been cleaned up, and there's a new ceramic tub in its place. Levi heads to his BMW.

The front door of the house opens again, and his dad comes out. "Don't talk to your mother that way," he yells.

Levi yanks the car door open and before he slides into the driver's seat, he glances up at my window.

I step back.

He caught me watching him on Saturday night and look where that led. Besides, I don't want him to think I'm spying on him.

Levi's car starts, and I move to the side of the window so I can peek out without him seeing me. He backs out of the driveway and his tyres squeal as he drives off down the street.

Levi's dad, Mark, stands on the veranda for a few minutes, staring after Levi's car. The way he has his hands clenched at his sides suggests he's not too happy with his son.

When he goes inside, I leave the window and grab my art history book from my bed. At my desk, I sit and turn to the section on Modernism, getting lost in the various artworks and making notes as I read. I can't concentrate for long though, and my mind keeps wandering to Levi, so I grab my journal, flip it open to a new page, and start writing.

I'm worried about Levi. He's ... being weird. His parents are yelling at him. He's yelling at them. He's drinking. I wish we were still friends so I could ask him what's going on. If I can do anything to help.

Then there's Veronica. Truth or dare ... such a stupid

game. I have no idea which one to choose. Maybe not thinking about it is best. Maybe I should just make a decision when and if I finally have to.

I sit back in my chair and stare at the page, chewing on the end of my pen. There are so many more thoughts I want to get down on paper, but my head is so full I don't know where to start.

The sound of a car engine brings me back to reality, and I glance at my clock. It's quarter past nine. I want to go to the window to see if it's Levi coming home, but I'm tired and I need to finish this chapter on Modernism before I turn in. I flip my journal closed and read for a few more minutes. I end up reading the same line five times.

I shake my head and laugh at myself. What is wrong with me? I've never been this distracted before when it comes to study.

I push my chair away from the desk and stare at the carpet beneath my feet. Using my toes to push off, I spin my chair around and around until I'm dizzy. Focussing on the dizziness helps me put everything out of my mind.

"I think the bougainvillea needs cutting back." Levi's voice startles me. His leg comes through the window, and he blurs as I spin. "It's hard to get my toes into the trellis."

I plant my feet on the floor and stop, gripping the sides of my seat. I stare at him and chew my bottom lip.

"Are you drunk this time? Because if you are, you can get out now."

"Nice to see you too, Katie."

"You could use the front door like a normal person." I scowl.

"That would take the fun out of it." Levi sits on the window seat with a goofy grin on his face. "Want me to spin you again?"

"What are you doing?" I stare at the open window behind him so I don't have to look into his eyes. They will undo me. "Why are you here?"

Levi runs a hand through his messy hair then stands and takes a step towards me. I roll my chair backwards until it hits my desk. Levi shoves his hands into his pockets and looks at his feet.

"Can we ... I want to ... Katie." His hand goes through his hair again and he lets out a long breath. "I want to apologise."

Levi looks up, and our eyes meet.

I take a deep breath. "Why?" My voice sounds small, like it has fallen into a huge canyon with me on one side and Levi on the other.

"Because ... Veronica hurt you. I want to make sure you're okay."

"Since when do you care?" I ask. "You made it perfectly clear the day I started at *your* school what you expect from me."

A light tap sounds on my bedroom door and I look at Levi with wide eyes. I jump up and yank the wardrobe door open, shoving him inside. The hangers clink together as he falls into them. My parents aren't that strict, but they still don't allow boys in my room, especially at this time of night.

"Katie, honey?" Mum pushes the door open and I meet her at the threshold. "Is everything okay? I heard voices."

"Fine, Mum." I pull my phone from my pocket. "I was

talking to Karen." She looks at my hand and frowns. "We hung up."

Mum opens the door wider. "Okay. Don't stay up too late."

Dad comes up the stairs and stops beside Mum. "You girls off to bed?"

"What's this? A family meeting?" Daniel sticks his head out of his room across the hall.

"Just saying goodnight," Mum says. "I'll see you two in the morning." She gives me a quick kiss. Dad ruffles my hair and follows Mum to their bedroom.

Daniel watches me from his doorway, waiting for Mum and Dad's door to close.

"Who's in there, Katie?" he whispers.

I chew the edge of my thumbnail. "Would you believe me if I said no one?"

He shakes his head and comes to my door, studying my room. "Bed or wardrobe?"

"Daniel …"

"You forget I'm two years older than you. If you've done it, I've probably done it a hundred times already."

"Please don't say anything."

Daniel chuckles and kisses me on the forehead. "Don't do anything stupid, but tell him if he hurts you, I'll break him." He says it loud enough so Levi can hear.

The door makes a soft click when I close it.

"You can come out now." I pick up the books from my bed and stack them on my desk. I sit near my pillow and cross my legs, hugging my favourite stuffed bunny to my chest.

The wardrobe door opens, and Levi sticks his head

out. "That was close."

"You're lucky I have an awesome brother."

"I know how great Daniel is. He and Mason ..." Levi shakes his head and comes to sit so he's facing me, one leg on the bed and the other resting so his foot is on the floor. He's quiet for a minute, staring at his hands. I really want him to leave, but I want him to stay, too.

"Katie—"

"You should go." I put my bunny in his place against the wall.

I don't need to hear what he has to say. No apology from him will fix the way Veronica treats me, or the way he has treated me, so what's the point? And being near him is exhausting. I can't handle the way I feel about him, because I love him and I hate him at the same time. It's too much.

"Can I stay and just ..." He shrugs. "I don't know, talk?"

"About what? I have nothing to say to you."

Levi pulls his other leg onto the bed and crosses them, mimicking me. "You were nice to me on Saturday night, even though—"

"You climbed up the side of my house and fell through my window. Drunk."

Levi sighs. "You're right. I should go."

He gets up from the bed and I do, too, but he hasn't stepped back to give me enough space. I stare at his chest. His T-shirt hugs the curves of his shoulders, and it's not until he clears his throat that I realise I've been staring too long. I drag my gaze away from him and look to the side towards the window. Heat rises in my cheeks and I fidget with the hem of my top, waiting for him to move.

He doesn't.

"I really am sorry," Levi says.

"You can't control Veronica's actions. But you can control your own." I finally get up the courage to look at him again. "Why are you friends with her?"

"Veronica is a tough nut, but she really can be nice. And we've been friends since year seven."

I laugh then clap my hand over my mouth. "If you think what she did to me is 'nice', then you're crazy." I move away from him, suddenly unable to breathe properly. "I've been your friend since birth, and you ditched me."

Levi sits on the bed again and rubs his face with his hands. I sit in my desk chair. It doesn't look like he's going to leave, so I swivel around and open my art history book to where I left off. We sit like that, in the quiet, for a while. I can feel him watching me, but I don't look in his direction.

When I realise I've read the same page three times over, I take my glasses off and clean them on the hem of my top. From the corner of my eye I catch Levi smiling, but I ignore him and put my glasses back on.

"You look nice without your specs," Levi says. "They hide your eyes."

Heat floods my cheeks and I let my hair fall across my face. "If you insist on staying, please be quiet."

Levi lies on the bed, his head on my pillow, and picks up my bunny. He plays with its ears, flopping them back and forth, before setting it back in its place. He folds his hands behind his head and stares at the ceiling.

"The stars up there," Levi says, "do they still glow?"

K. A. LAST

"I said, quiet."

"Okay, okay. I can handle quiet. It's a refreshing change."

The tone of his voice hints at sadness, and I wonder what's getting him down.

There seems to be something going on with his family, but how do I ask him if he's okay when we haven't been close for so long? It's been a while since Mason died, and we never talked about it, because when it happened, Levi had already cut me off. Maybe he just misses his brother. Even though I'd gone to the funeral, and I'd wanted to offer him my condolences, I didn't know how. I figured he wouldn't have wanted to talk to me anyway. Maybe I should talk to him about it now, because if it was me and I'd lost Daniel, no amount of time would ever fix the pain.

"Where were you this afternoon?" I ask, keeping my eyes on my text book.

Levi rolls onto his side and props himself up on his elbow. "Headmistress's office. Then I came home."

When I look at him, his eyes are cast down at the doona cover. He runs his finger around the edge of one of the butterflies in the pattern.

"Mrs Pritchard questioned me about ..." He raises his head and points to his cheek.

I sit back in my chair and swivel to face him. "What did you tell her?"

"I fell over and face-planted the garden path." He drops his gaze back to the bed. "I don't think she believed me."

"But that's exactly what you did."

"Apparently, they think I was in a fight, or someone hit me."

"That's … crazy. Isn't it?"

Levi locks his gaze on mine. "Not so crazy if you've been through what my family has."

"Do you want to talk about … you know?"

"You mean Mason?"

I stay quiet. Yes, I mean Mason, but I don't want to push him. I'm glad we're talking again, even though it is in secret, and I don't want him to clam up on me.

"It's okay. We don't have to talk about him." I rub my knees with my hands, then twist my fingers together. Levi stays silent. "Did Veronica tell you what else she did to me today?"

"There's more?" Levi sits and swings his legs over the edge of the bed.

"Truth or dare." I stare at him.

His mouth opens. "She didn't."

"She did."

We stare at each other, and I have no idea what to say next. I want to ask him if he'll play with me now. I have so many questions I want answered, but I don't think he'll agree.

"What did you tell her?"

"I haven't told her anything," I say. "And I'm not going to."

Levi stands up. "No, Katie. You can't do that. You think Ronnie was bad today? You have no idea what she's capable of."

"Yeah, I do. I was there when Karen got suspended. Remember?"

"You have to choose." He sits down again.

"I don't want to."

"Now is not the time to be stubborn."

"Come on, Levi," I say. "What's the worst she can do to me?"

"She can ruin your reputation."

I laugh. "What reputation?"

Levi goes quiet and stares at me, his brow knitted. He presses his lips together and rubs his face with his hand.

He sits on the edge of the bed, his back straight, and puts his hands on his knees. "What would you choose if I asked you?"

"What? No. I'm not choosing."

"Come on, Katie. Truth or dare?"

I stare at him, my mouth slightly open, unsure what to say. A moment ago, I wanted to play with him, but this could go in my favour or it could all go terribly wrong. On the other hand, if he truth or dares me, then I can do it back to him.

"I'll do this on one condition," I say. "You play, too."

"Okay." Levi waits, and his eyes bore into me.

"Dare." My heart pounds. *What have I done?*

Levi raises his eyebrows. "Is that what you would have chosen for Veronica?"

"I'm not answering that. Now dare me to do something."

"Stand up." Levi gets to his feet and takes my hand, pulling me from my chair. "I dare you to kiss me."

A puff of air leaves my mouth and I go tense. I pull my fingers from Levi's grasp. *What the hell?*

He smirks, and I want to punch him.

"You want me to kiss you?"

"No. Yes. Maybe." Levi laughs. "I want you to think your way around the dare. There's always an out. A way for you to complete the dare, but not in the way the person who dares you is expecting. So … Kiss me."

I bite my lip and step towards Levi. His lips are slightly parted and the white of his teeth peeks through. I've fantasised about kissing him a million times, and now he's dared me to, I want to so badly, but I also know that it's not the real reason he's dared me to do it.

I push up with my toes and plant a soft kiss on his cheek. His stubble scratches my lips, and his pine scent makes me a little dizzy. I grab his forearms to stop myself from falling into him.

"Does that count?" I ask.

"That totally counts." He grins, and I can't help grinning, too.

I sit back in my chair before my knees buckle and I fall over.

We're quiet for a few minutes. I try to take even breaths because my heart is hammering so fast Levi must be able to hear it.

"I should say dare to Veronica," I say. "But what if it's something I can't get around like I did … kissing you?"

"You could always take truth, and then lie." Levi shrugs. "She'll want to embarrass you no matter which way you go."

"But I'm a terrible liar. And what if she asks me something I can't lie about?" I press my lips together. "I'll think on it. But now it's your turn. Truth or dare, Levi?"

He lies back on my bed, taking up the same position as before with his hands tucked behind his head. He crosses his legs at the ankles and looks up at the ceiling. "Truth."

I sit up straighter. I wasn't expecting him to choose truth. I figured he'd go with the dare because he'd think I was too nice to ask him to do anything horrible.

I sift through my thoughts, and all the questions I've wanted to ask him over the years, trying to find the one I want answered the most. This could be my only chance to get something from him. Something other than rejection.

I take a deep breath, and finally ask, "Do you ever think we can be friends again?"

Levi turns to look at me. A small smile plays at his lips and I want to look away because I'm embarrassed, but I hold his gaze.

"I thought you'd ask me why I did what I did to you," he says.

"I know why you did it, Levi."

I hold my breath, waiting for his answer, and I realise I'm not really sure what I want it to be. But maybe it's not a question of what I want, but rather, what I need.

"Yes, Katie." Levi's smile widens. "My answer is yes."

4

That bitch will never see you coming

The rest of the first week back at school goes by quickly. Veronica pretty much leaves me alone all week, bar a few snide comments and occasional death stares, and Levi does, too. The latter I'm not very happy about, especially since he told me we could be friends again.

I'm guessing he didn't mean straight away.

Levi doesn't climb in my window again all week, and the most I get from him in the halls is a nod or a close-lipped smile. The more I think about him, the more things I find to be annoyed about. He obviously doesn't remember the conversation we had when he climbed in my window drunk, because he hasn't asked for any help with study. And now, it's the weekend, and only one week until trial exams.

A bang pulls me from my thoughts.

"Katie?" Dad says.

I shake my head and stare at my father, then at the garden rake resting at a funny angle against the side of the house.

"Sorry, what?" I bend and retrieve the tool I'd been using.

Dad chuckles. "Where did you go? Lost you for a minute there."

"Just thinking." I rake some bougainvillea clippings away from the side of the house.

"Tell me again why you want this thing cut back?" Dad hacks at a particularly stubborn branch.

"They scratch the house at night," I say. "It's ... creepy."

Which is the best excuse I can come up with. I'm not about to tell Dad I want easier access for Levi to climb up to my bedroom. *If* he ever does again.

A door slams, and I turn towards Levi's house. He's standing on his veranda, watching Dad prune the plant that clings to the trellis on the side of our house. Levi jumps down the steps in two leaps and heads towards us, a lopsided grin on his face.

"Morning, Katie, Bill. Need any help?" he asks.

I stare at him with wide eyes. What the hell is he doing?

Dad stops cutting and holds the sheers at his side. "I think I've got it covered. How are you, Levi?" Dad's forehead creases, and he throws me a questioning glace before turning back to torment the bougainvillea.

"Fine, thanks." Levi rocks on his heels. "Katie, can I talk to you?"

I don't want to talk to him. He's avoided me most of

the week, and I'm not about to let him think he can just come over here and be all 'oh, we're friends again' when none of his mates are around to see.

I chew my lip and frown, then turn and walk away before my mouth opens and something comes out that I'll probably regret, or that I shouldn't say in front of my dad.

Levi follows me to the front door, and when I try to close the screen he jams his foot in the gap.

"Katie, what's the matter?" he asks.

"Please leave." How can I explain to him that I'm hurt and angry when he probably won't even know why?

"Did you ask your dad to cut the bougainvillea back?"

"You haven't spoken to me all week," I say.

"I ..." He frowns. "It's not that simple."

"Really?" I yank the screen door so it squashes his foot.

A silver Subaru pulls into Levi's driveway, and the driver honks the horn. Levi glances over his shoulder then pulls his foot from the door. It slams shut because I'm still pulling on the handle. I glare at him through the mesh.

Jarred gets out of the car and leans against the bonnet.

"Go on," I say. "Better not let him see you over here. Who knows what rumours might spread?"

Levi turns back to me, his jaw clenched. I can't look at him, so I slam our heavy front door in his face.

"What's all the noise about?" Mum calls from the kitchen.

"Nothing." I race upstairs to my room and slam that door, too.

From my open window I look down onto the yard. Levi talks to Dad, then helps him put a few branches into the garden bin. He jogs over to Jarred who has moved to the veranda steps. They clap each other on the back in that stupid way guys do. Jarred says something while looking up at my window, and I quickly draw the curtains before stepping back.

The room is darker, but I don't mind. It matches my mood. I flop onto my bed and grab my bunny, hugging it to my chest. Why do people have to suck so much?

My journal is sitting on the edge of my desk so I reach over and grab it. It's funny because I'm not sure what I want to write down, but when my pen hits the paper the words come more easily than I thought they would.

He tells me we can be friends again, then he ignores me! What a joke. Why did I even bother getting my hopes up? I don't fit in Levi's world anymore. Did I ever really fit there in the first place?

The whole 'truth or dare' thing is eating at me, too. Why do they make such a big deal of playing a game where the only objective is to humiliate people? If I choose truth, what will Veronica ask me? What if it's something I can't lie convincingly about? What if it's Something about Levi? I'm not sure if I could ever be prepared to answer any questions to do with him. If I choose dare, it might be embarrassing, but at least I won't have to bare my soul.

My phone vibrates on my desk and I reach over to grab it. Karen's name flashes on the screen with a picture of her I took when we went bowling a few months ago. I'm not sure I'm in the mood for talking at the moment. All I feel like doing is wallowing in self-pity.

I swipe the screen anyway. "Hey, you."

"Hey. I was about to hang up," Karen says. "Why so gloomy?"

"Levi was just here."

"Get. Out! Why?"

I'm not sure how to answer. She sounds as surprised as I was when Levi fell through my window a week ago. We've been best friends for a long time. Karen knows all there is to know about what's happened and hasn't happened between Levi and me. Except for the stuff I haven't told her about this week.

"He saw Dad cutting the bougainvillea back and came over. Then he offered to help."

"Why is your dad cutting back …?" Karen squeals. "Oh my God. Did he?"

"Did he what?" I ask, knowing full well what she means.

"Did he climb in your window?"

"He … might have."

Karen squeals again. "Oh my God!"

"Stop saying that. It's not as big a deal as you think. The guy's a jerk."

"So, you didn't talk to him just now?"

"No," I say. "I told him to leave me alone, and then I slammed the door in his face."

"Oh, Katie." Karen sighs.

"Jarred turned up, and he saw Levi talking to me. The minute that happened, Levi changed back to the rich kid who's too good to be seen with me."

Karen groans. "I really don't like Jarred."

"You're using nice words. That's unlike you."

"I'm saving all the bad ones for the next time he's a dick to you."

I smile. I love how Karen can make me feel so much better just by talking to me about stupid stuff. But I also can't help wondering why some people are like they are. Why do people like Jarred and Veronica single out people like me and Karen? I guess it's a power thing, but I just don't get it. What did I ever do to make them hate me? I mind my own business, but because I'm not rich like them I'm a target.

"Why do you think Veronica hates me so much?" I ask Karen.

"She's jealous."

"That's funny. Of what? I'm not rich. I don't have a car. I'm hardly a supermodel—"

"Stop right there," Karen says. "You're beautiful. And you're smart. And Levi is your next-door neighbour. There are plenty of things for Veronica to be jealous about. You know, because you've got me as a best friend, too."

I burst out laughing and fall back onto my bed, putting my hand over my mouth. "Yep, she'd definitely be jealous of that."

Mum used to tell me people picked on others because they liked them, but I stopped believing that by the time I got to high school.

"What are you doing today?" Karen asks.

"Apart from butchering my favourite plant, studying."

"Get ready—we're going out. I'll pick you up in fifteen."

"What? No. I don't want to go anywhere."

Something

"Come on, Katie," Karen pleads. "We'll go to the shops. I'll buy you a hot chocolate. We'll window shop. It'll be fun."

I roll over on my pillow and rest my ear on my phone. The last thing I feel like doing is following Karen around the shops. But I could use the company, and I'm not sure I can focus on study anyway, not after my encounter with Levi.

"Okay," I say. "I'll see you soon."

I stand in front of my wardrobe for ten minutes and still can't decide what to wear. Late July is always chilly, but I know I'll get hot traipsing around the shops. I opt for the jeans I already have on, and the prettiest top I own—a turquoise number with little pink flowers on it. It's sleeveless, so I grab my favourite cream cardigan and hope I won't be too cold.

I rip the elastic out of my hair and fluff it a bit so it sits around my shoulders, then I coat my lips with gloss, and adjust my glasses, wishing I didn't need them.

I take them off for a second and stare at my face in the full-length mirror on my wardrobe door, remembering what Levi said about my glasses hiding my eyes. With a sigh, I put them back on. There's no reason for me to listen to him. It's not like I need to impress him. He's not my boyfriend.

A car horn honks, and I run to the window. Karen is sitting behind the wheel of her mum's car, stopped at the kerb. I shove my feet into my worn black Converse, grab my tote, and slip my wallet, phone, and cardigan inside, then run downstairs to the kitchen.

"Mum? I'm going to the shops with Karen."

"Okay, honey." She looks up from where she's sitting

at the kitchen counter, reading a magazine. "Have fun."

I grab my house keys from the bowl on the hall table and head outside. Levi and Jarred are leaning on Jarred's car, talking. They stop as soon as they see me, but I don't make eye contact with them.

Dad puts down his pruning shears and meets me at the kerb. "Where are you girls off to, Katie?"

"We're going to the shops." I glance around the yard. "You don't need me?"

"Nah, you go and have fun. Just be home for dinner."

"Hey," Karen says through her open window.

"Hi, Karen," Dad says. He smiles, then pulls his wallet from his back pocket, taking out a twenty and handing it to me.

I'm aware of Levi and Jarred watching us, but I resist the urge to look at them. "Dad, no. I don't need any money."

"You're the strangest teenager, Katie. Take it. You can buy yourself some lunch."

I give him a kiss on the cheek and stuff the money in my tote bag. I hate taking money from my parents. We don't have much, and everything that's spare they use to make up the difference for my education. The scholarship only covers so much. But I don't want to make a scene in front of Levi and Jarred. I resist the urge again to look in their direction. Levi's stare melts me, like hot lava. Or at least it feels that way. I have no idea if he's actually looking.

"Someone's checking you out," Karen says as I slide into the passenger seat.

He's looking!

"He's not checking me out. He's probably plotting

something humiliating. Something to dare me for when I finally answer Veronica."

"You're going to accept the dare? Not take truth?" Karen asks.

I look at my best friend and try to catch a glimpse of Levi from the corner of my eye. "I don't know what I'm going to do yet."

Karen blatantly looks in Levi and Jarred's direction. "He's totally watching you."

"Is not."

"Is too. Because you're hot."

"I'm cold, actually." I pull my cardigan from my bag and slip it on before buckling my seatbelt. "And Levi never felt that way about me. If he did, he never would have dumped me as a friend."

"Then why is he looking at you as if he could eat you up?"

"Karen! I am the last person Levi wants. Would you just … drive?"

Karen frowns and puts her mum's Suzuki Swift into first. "Okay then. Let's get some retail therapy. Shopping fixes everything."

It takes us twenty minutes to get to the closest Westfield shopping centre. Karen cranks the music and we sing along at the top of our lungs.

Karen parks the car and we make our way through the steady stream of shoppers, past the smaller shops and outside to the mall towards our favourite café. We grab a takeaway hot chocolate each before heading back inside.

"We should look for formal dresses," Karen says.

"I thought we were going to do that with Jess and Stacey."

"They won't mind." Karen slips her arm through mine. "We can all go shopping again another weekend."

I follow Karen around for an hour. She lives for this kind of thing, but I can never really get into it. What's the point when I can't afford to buy anything anyway?

I let Karen ooh and aah over all the pretty dresses. She tries a couple on, and my stomach growls as Karen changes out of a deep purple pencil dress.

She opens the stall door, her eyebrows raised. "Lunch?"

I nod. "I'd love to find a dress that colour for the formal. Or something with purple in it at least."

Karen puts the dress back on the hanger. "This cut won't suit you. But we'll find something else."

We give the dresses back to the sales lady, who frowns, and giggle as we leave the shop.

"Not sure we should go back there," I say.

"Yes, we will. There are a few dresses I think you should try on. But first, food." Karen pulls me in the direction of the food court. When we get there, most of the seats are taken. We spot one free table in the middle, so Karen runs off to save it while I line up.

At the pizza place, I pass the few minutes I have to stand there by glancing around the food court. My heart beats faster when I spot Levi and Jarred on the other side, lined up for burgers. I wipe my sweaty palms on my jeans and face the front of the line, hoping they haven't seen me.

I'm almost at the front when I feel someone's presence behind me.

Something

"I hear the pepperoni is really good," Levi says.

I turn to look at him.

Levi rocks on his heels, one hand gripping a takeaway paper bag, the other stuffed into the pocket of his jeans. He glances over his shoulder, his gaze darting around as if he's looking for someone.

I stare at him in disbelief. "Are you feeling okay?" I ask before I can stop myself.

"Fine. Why?"

I glance around. "Aren't you worried Jarred will see you talking to me?"

"He's gone to the bathroom."

I eye Levi sideways. Just because Jarred is in the bathroom doesn't mean he won't see us. Boys pee really fast. I'm pretty sure he'll be back soon. I have no idea why I'm so worried though. It's not like *my* reputation is on the line.

I step up to the counter and order two slices of vegetarian pizza and some garlic bread. Asking Levi what he wants is on the tip of my tongue, but I stay silent. Right now, I don't really trust myself not to say something stupid or mean. And I don't want to be either of those people.

After paying for my food, I walk away from Levi towards Karen. Levi follows, and I'm not sure what to do. Telling him to go away crosses my mind, but I decide to let this play out and see what happens.

Karen's eyes widen when she sees who is walking behind me, and I give her my best 'please keep your mouth shut' look, hoping she'll understand what I'm asking of her from my contorted facial expression. I slide the tray with our pizza on it onto the table and sit down across from her.

Levi glances around again, his jaw clenched, and his lips pressed together. My stomach churns with anger and I don't feel so hungry anymore.

"If you're worried about someone seeing you with us, then why don't you go away?" I ask.

I hate that he can make me feel this way, and I wish it didn't affect me so much. I want things between us to be like they used to, but I need to wake up, because it's never going to happen. Levi was everything to me. Now he's just a guy I used to be friends with. I can't keep kidding myself and thinking everything will magically go back to how it was. I want him back, but at the same time, I want him to go away so I can breathe.

"What do you want, Levi?" Karen asks, then takes a bite from her pizza.

Mine sits in front of me untouched. I grab my garlic bread and tear a piece off, but I don't eat it.

"Um ... I ..." Levi sets his paper bag on the table and runs a hand through his hair, making my insides flip. "Katie, I ..."

"Oh my God, spit it out," Karen says.

Levi pulls a chair over from the table next to us and sits down. "Exams are next week. I was wondering if ... you know?"

"You want me to help you study?" I don't look at him. I stare at my garlic bread and the film of butter on my fingertips.

"Only if it's no trouble."

I finally look at him. "Sure."

"Okay then. Thanks." Levi stands and grabs his lunch.

Something

"You better shoo before Jarred catches you talking to us and the world ends." Karen waves her hand at him, then goes back to eating her pizza. Levi walks away, and Karen watches him from the corner of her eye until he's out of hearing range. Then she turns on me. "What the hell?"

"You know how I told you—"

"Levi climbed in your window?"

"Yeah ... well, I also offered to tutor him for History." I shove the piece of garlic bread in my mouth so I don't have to talk anymore.

Food in her mouth doesn't stop Karen. "That means you can spend more time with him," she says through a mouthful of pizza.

"It's not a big deal." I wipe my hands on a paper napkin.

"You're kidding me, right? Has he climbed in your window more than once?"

I raise my eyebrows. "Maybe."

Karen sits forward in her chair. "You're going to tell me everything, and we're not moving until you're done."

"Twice. He's climbed up twice. The first time he was drunk, and ... it's a long story."

Karen glares at me. "I don't care if we have to sit here until tomorrow. Spill."

"You know how he hurt his face? Well, he fell down the veranda steps. His mum was pretty upset." I stop and think back to the night Levi climbed up the second time. He hadn't been drunk, but he had been angry. "The second time I think he'd had a fight with his dad. There was yelling."

"Did he tell you what the fight was about?" Karen asks.

"No ... but we did play truth or dare." I stare at my best friend. "He dared me to kiss him, and I asked him if we would ever be friends again."

"Get. Out!" Karen hits me on the arm, then sits back in her chair. "What did you do? What did he say?"

"I kissed him, and he said yes."

Karen's mouth hangs open. "You kissed—"

"Don't get too excited—it was on the cheek. He wanted to prove a point."

"Being?" Karen rolls her hand through the air.

"That there's an out for every dare. You just have to think of a way to do what you've been dared to do, but not how the darer is expecting."

Karen raises her eyebrows. "Veronica?"

I nod. "I think I'm going to choose dare."

Karen laughs. "That bitch will never see you coming."

5

The bed can be Switzerland if you like

evi didn't climb in my window on Monday night like I expected him to. A little bit of hope fell away on Tuesday when he didn't show. On Wednesday, I tried to ignore the empty feeling in my stomach when I turned my light out at ten pm and he hadn't come. By Thursday, I'd given up completely, and I spent the night at Karen's place, studying with her.

On Friday, I was pretty pissed off with Levi.

And Veronica had been giving me hell all week, pushing me for an answer. The more she pushed, the more I didn't want to give her one.

Now, the last bell for the day rings and I pack up my math books. Double Math on a Friday afternoon is pure torture, especially when all we've been doing is revision for the past two weeks. Exams start on Monday, and I think I'm ready, but I'm nervous, too. Everything I've worked so hard for starts now. Everyone keeps telling me I'll get dux, but I've been so distracted that I'm not as confident as I have been in the past. Maybe writing my speech was a waste of time.

I shoulder my bag, and head out to meet Karen.

"Why so blue?" she asks as I walk towards her. She's leaning against a tree on the nature strip outside the gate.

"It is that obvious?" I hug my folder to my chest as if it's a shield.

"Your face is all screwed up."

"Thanks." I laugh.

"That's better. Come on. I don't want to miss the train."

We hit the footpath to start our ten-minute walk up the hill when a horn blares.

"Hey, Katie," Veronica yells.

I turn towards the sound of her voice. She's across the street, hanging out the back driver's side window of Levi's BMW.

I take a deep breath and stop on the kerb. "Yes, Veronica?"

"Get in." She thumbs over her shoulder to indicate I should cross the road and get in the car.

She's crazy.

"I'm fine, thanks." I slip my arm through Karen's and start walking again.

"What are you doing?" Karen whispers. "Get in the car."

I stop. "What? No."

"Katie." Levi's voice travels across the street.

"He wants you to get in," Karen says.

"I'm not getting into his car." I clench my teeth.

"He hasn't climbed in your window all week. So yes,

you are." Karen spins me around so I'm facing Levi.

"You want a ride?" He raises his eyebrows, and my stomach flutters.

Why does he have to look so hot? And be so irresistible?

"If you give Karen a lift, too, then yes," I say.

"Sure. Hop in."

I pull Karen across the street.

"I really don't need to come," she says.

"I'm not leaving you here."

We reach the other side of the road, and Jarred gets out of the front passenger seat, a scowl on his face. He leaves his door open and puts his hand out for me to get in. If he didn't look so angry, I would have called it a gentlemanly move. He yanks the back door open and climbs in.

Karen stoops so she's staring at Veronica. "I'm not sitting in the back with her."

"Get in, bitch," she says.

"Just ... get in, Karen," I say.

I dump my bag in the foot well, slide into the front passenger seat, and pull the door closed. I look at Levi and he smiles. I shake my head. His smile drops away.

I turn and look at Veronica. "You call Karen a bitch again and I'll—"

"What?" Veronica asks. "What will you do, bitch?"

"Ronnie, that's enough," Levi says. He gives her a death stare in the rear-view mirror. It makes me feel a little better, but I'm itching to say something back to her.

On the way home, I gaze out the window because I don't want to look at Levi. When I'm this close to him, my anger is replaced with hope. If I look at him, that hope will probably turn to longing, and then I'll be done for.

I catch sight of Karen in the side mirror. She pulls a funny face and I giggle.

"Care to share?" Veronica asks.

"Not with you," I say.

Karen bursts out laughing.

"What?" Veronica asks. "What's so funny?"

I turn in my seat, and the scowl on Veronica's face makes her look ugly. She's quite pretty, and if she smiled more it would do her the world of good.

"Wouldn't you like to know?" I say.

"Can you drive faster, Levi? I need to get out of this car," Jarred says.

He's squashed between Karen and Veronica, and seeing how uncomfortable he is makes me laugh harder.

"I'm not having much fun either," Karen says, through fits of giggles.

"Sounds like you are." Levi glances at me.

I stop laughing and go back to staring out the window.

Levi turns off the highway down a wide tree-lined street, taking the first right and then the next left. He stops outside a house that would fit mine in it three times.

"Catch you bitches later." Veronica throws her door open. She gets out and comes to my window, rolling her hand for me to wind it down.

I press the electric button and the window whirs. "What?"

"Truth or dare, Katie?"

"Give it a rest," I say. "You'll get your answer when I'm ready."

"I want it now." She leans down and puts her hand

on the car, gripping the edge of the door through the open window.

"Well, we don't always get what we want." I stare at her. I'm tired of letting her intimidate me. It's time to give her a taste of her own medicine.

She clenches her teeth. "When, then?"

I tap my cheek as if in thought, raising my eyebrows. "After exams."

"That's two weeks away!"

"Yep."

"Take it or leave it," Karen says from the back seat.

"This is *not* how it works." Veronica straightens. "Tell her, Levi. We don't play this way."

"I do," I say. "If you want my answer, you'll have to wait."

"Let it go, Ronnie." Levi grips the steering wheel.

"Whatever." Veronica turns around and walks up the path leading to her house, or rather, her mansion.

We drive again, taking a few more right and left turns until I'm lost, and we drop Jarred off. His place is just as flashy as Veronica's, complete with swimming pool and tennis court. My house looks like a shack in comparison.

Since I started private school, I've learnt that there are three kinds of people: the rich ones, the not as rich, and then there's me. Levi is somewhere in the middle of the rich and the not as rich, but he has looks and charm, so everyone loves him. Karen is at the lower end of the not as rich, and I'm the one who could only afford private school on a scholarship.

Thinking about the class distinctions upsets me, so I go back to staring out the window, waiting for this stupid car ride to be over. Suddenly, I don't want to be anywhere near Levi, and I can't believe I ever got into the car with him in the first place.

"Can we just go home, please?" I lean my elbow on the open window and rest my head against the seat.

We turn back onto the highway. Karen's place isn't far from mine and Levi's, and it's on the way. When we stop at the kerb, she unbuckles her seatbelt and leans forward between the two front seats.

"You need to stop being a dick, Levi, and pull your head out of your arse."

Levi and I both turn to the middle to look at my best friend. My mouth hangs open, ready to give her a serve, but Levi talks first.

"You're right." He glances at me. "I am a dick, and a jerk, and an arse, too." He smiles.

"Okay, then." Karen opens her door and gets out. She walks backwards up her path with her bag hanging from one hand. She points two fingers at her eyes, and then at Levi.

"I have no doubt she's watching me," Levi says, quietly.

"She's always had my back." I lean my head against the seat again and close my eyes. I don't want to see the expression on Levi's face, but I hope he gets that I'm angry with him. I have to take a deep breath, because thinking about it and being so close to him makes me really sad. Can I ever trust him? If we do fix our friendship like he said we could, how will I know he won't hurt me all over again? Am I setting myself up for another disaster?

The car turns and comes to a stop. "We're home."

I open my eyes and stare at Levi's house. "Thanks for the lift."

Something

He kills the engine and jumps out, coming around to my side of the car before I've managed to get my bag and folder sorted. Levi opens the door and takes my bag from me. I frown but let him help me out of the car.

We stand on the driveway, looking everywhere but at each other.

"Can I have my bag?" I clutch my folder to my chest.

Levi hands it to me. "You, um …" He glances at his front door. "Want to come inside?"

I look over to my house, and I feel like running straight up to my room, and never speaking to him again. I want my safe place, and right now being with Levi is not it.

I push my glasses up my nose and tuck my hair behind my ear.

"We can study," Levi says.

I laugh. "You want to study now? Exams start on Monday. It's a bit late."

"History is my worst subject. I should be fine with the others."

"Well, you should've come study with me before."

Levi smiles, but it doesn't reach his eyes. "It's okay. I can do it on my own." He turns and heads for the veranda. I wait until his foot hits the top step.

"Levi," I call out. "Mum and Dad won't be home until later. I've got an hour or so."

He turns, his smile widening. "Okay."

"Okay."

I take a deep breath and follow Levi into the foyer of his house.

His mum has it decorated like a show home. It's always been like that, but it's been so long since I've stepped foot inside that the clinical feeling surprises me. There's no warmth. It doesn't feel like a home. It's just a house.

I glance up the stairs to the second storey. Levi's bedroom door is open. I try to remember the last time I was in his room, and I can't.

"Want something to drink?" Levi asks.

I nod and follow him into the kitchen, dumping my bag on the huge timber dining table that sits in the open-plan family room. Levi opens the fridge, and I pull up one of the bar stools at the kitchen bench.

"Coke? Lemonade?" He looks at me around the fridge door.

"Water, thanks."

Levi brings out a jug of chilled water and a can of Coke, then sets them on the bench. He pops the can and takes a swig, grabs a glass from the cupboard in the corner, and pours me a water. We stare at each other across the bench, and I can't help thinking that even though we're so close physically, he still feels so far away. I want to close the gap, but I'm not sure how.

I sip my water. "So ... why do you struggle with History?"

Levi puts his can down and leans on the bench with both hands. "I can never remember all the details."

"It's not that difficult. You just have to associate what you want to remember with something already familiar."

Levi raises his eyebrows. "How?"

"It's called the Roman Room method. You choose a room in your house you know really well, then you pick an object and use it to associate certain pieces of information."

Levi stands up straight and folds his arms. "A room in my house?"

Something

"It can be any room. For instance, my bed is Pompeii, and my pillow is Vesuvius. And each of my soft toys is assigned a piece of information."

"You made your bed Pompeii?"

I laugh. "It's a really easy and effective technique. You should try it."

Levi walks to the door that leads back into the foyer. "Come on then. Let's go make my bed Pompeii."

I hesitate and bite my lip. "You don't want to study down here?"

"My room is the room I know the best." He leans against the doorjamb. "The bed can be Switzerland if you like."

6

Bring it, bitch

$\mathcal{W}$e didn't end up going to Levi's bedroom. I told him I was more comfortable studying at his kitchen bench, and he didn't push me. For some reason, the thought of being in his room was different to having him in mine—maybe because it's out of my comfort zone.

Exams fly past in a two-week haze of study at night and information regurgitation during the day. The weekend in between is filled with more study, and Levi has mastered the climb up the trellis. He comes over most nights, and we fall into a routine of two hours on the books followed by an hour of talking.

Levi also drives me to school some mornings. He offers to do it every day, but I tell him I'm not about to completely ditch Jessica and Karen. I secretly hope he finds some meaning in that. Veronica is horrified on the mornings

Something

I'm in the car before her, but she mostly leaves me alone. Other than reminding me I owe her an answer after our last exam.

I haven't forgotten.

Now, it's the last day of exams, and thinking about Veronica is making me ill. I don't want today to end, because I don't want to choose. But I will, because I'm not afraid of her, and I said I would.

Dad watches me from across the table.

"Why are you looking at me funny?" I take a bite of my toast.

"No reason." He adjusts his morning paper and it rustles. "What's the deal with you and Levi?"

My mouth hangs open. "What do you mean? We're just friends."

"Maybe. When you were ten. I've seen the way he looks at you. I was a teenager once, too, you know."

I look at Mum, but she shrugs and takes a big gulp of coffee, raising her eyebrows over the top of her cup.

"Well, there's no *deal*. We're—"

"Just friends?" Daniel saunters into the kitchen and grabs a banana from the fruit bowl.

Dad sips his coffee and feigns thoughtfulness. "Cutting back the bougainvillea had nothing to do with access to the trellis then?"

I almost choke on my toast. "I ... what? ... No!"

Mum tries to hide a smirk with a hand over her mouth.

Dad sets his paper down and places his hands on the table. "Katie, honey, I know he's climbed in your window more than once, and he's lucky I haven't strangled him."

"But ... he used to do it all the time when we were

younger."

"That was before he started looking at you like ..." Dad takes a deep breath. "Do we need to have the facts-of-life talk again?"

"Oh my God, no!" I say. Daniel laughs, and I glare at him. "Did you tell them?"

"You knew about this?" Dad stands.

Daniel's eyes go wide. "Dad, calm down. We should trust Katie."

"Yes, we should," I say. "There's nothing going on other than study."

"Well, this is my warning, Katie." Dad points a finger at me. "He's a teenage boy, so if he comes over he has to use the front door. And if I catch him in your room when I don't know about it, there will be hell to pay."

"Your father is right," Mum says. "Climbing in your window isn't the right thing to do. But it is romantic."

"Whose side are you on?" Dad asks.

"I'm just saying." Mum smiles. "He obviously likes you, Katie." She stands and clears our breakfast dishes, taking them to the sink.

"We've all known Levi for a very long time," Dad says. "He's a good kid, but he's been through a lot, and he's hurt you in the past. I want you to be careful."

"I will." My voice is small, because Dad is right.

Dad takes his work jacket from the back of his chair and puts it on. "Do you have a crush on him?"

What can I say? I've never been a good liar. "Yes. But Dad, we're just friends. He doesn't think of me like that."

"Oh, let me assure you, he does. Now, I'm going to work." Dad kisses Mum on the cheek and gives me a kiss

Something

on the head on his way past.

I pick at my fingernails and wait until Dad leaves before talking again. "Mum, how can I tell if he's really interested?"

"Climbing in your bedroom window is a sure sign." Daniel takes a bite from his banana.

Mum sighs and leans against the bench. "I know that look he has, Katie. I've seen it in your father's eyes. We don't want to have to put restrictions on you, or tell you who you can and can't see. We trust you, honey, but he needs to use the front door."

"Okay."

There's a knock at the door, and Daniel goes to get it. A second later, he calls out, "Katie, Levi's here."

Mum and I exchange a glance and she smiles. "Good luck today." She comes over and gives me a hug.

"Thanks, Mum." I grab my bag on the way out of the kitchen.

Levi stands on the threshold, leaning against the doorjamb with his hands in his pockets.

"Big day today, Katie," he says. "You ready?"

"If you're talking about exams, yes." I shoulder my bag and we walk outside to Levi's car. "If you mean Veronica, then no."

"Are you going to tell me what you've decided?" Levi opens the front passenger door for me.

I slide into the seat and dump my bag in the foot well then look up at him. "That would also be a no. Stop asking me. You've asked a million times over the past couple of weeks."

"You're no fun." He closes my door, goes around to the

driver's side, and gets in. "I won't tell anyone."

"You'll find out when she does." I smile. It's nice to have something over him. "Not long to wait."

Levi starts the car. "You've drawn this out longer than anyone else has ever gotten away with."

"I won't let her intimidate me. She needs to learn she won't always get what she wants when she wants it."

"She's nicer than you think, you know."

Levi backs out of the driveway and we start the drive to school. I frown but settle into the seat and try to focus on something other than Veronica. She'll be in the car soon, and I should probably be as calm as possible.

We pick Jarred up first. He grunts when he gets in, and I think that's the extent of the conversation I'll have with him this morning. Levi stops outside Veronica's place a few minutes later, and she yanks the door open.

"I want the front seat back." She flops into the car and pouts.

"Good morning," I say.

"It'll be better this afternoon when you give me my answer."

I turn in my seat to look at her. "It's killing you, isn't it?"

"You know, I could've burnt you by now."

"Why haven't you?" I raise my eyebrows.

Veronica's gaze flicks quickly to Levi, she smirks then stares out the window and doesn't answer. I turn back to face the front. What did the look she gave him mean? Is he involved somehow? He has pestered me quite a bit to tell him what I'm going to say.

My stomach fills with a sinking feeling, and by the time we reach school, I think I'm going to vomit. What if Levi is in on whatever Veronica has in store for me? What if him being nice is all just a show so the letdown will be worse for me, and far more fun for everyone else?

I open my door before Levi has the chance to turn the car off. "I'm going to find Karen." I jump out and cross the street before he can stop me.

I walk quickly up the back driveway into school, and don't look to see if Levi and the others have followed. Karen reaches our lockers a minute after I do—just enough time for me to empty my bag of everything I don't need for our last exam.

"Hey," Karen says. "I miss anything this morning?"

I slam my locker shut. "Just the usual."

"Veronica?" Karen asks.

"I don't really want to talk about it." All I want to do is focus on getting through today.

"I could beat her up for you."

I laugh, and look Karen up and down. "No, you couldn't."

"Well, I could try."

"Please don't. As annoying as you are sometimes, I actually like you."

Karen grins and we head to the hall for our last trial exam. If we get there before Levi and Veronica, I can find a seat at the front and put my head down with no distractions.

Karen and I walk through the big doors at the back of the hall and make our way to the front row of seats. There are already quite a few students in here, and we're lucky to get the last two desks on the side at the front. I chuckle to myself because only I would think getting a seat at the front is lucky.

No sooner have I sat than I can sense his presence. I don't know what it is about Levi, but I always feel him when he walks into a room, or if he's close by. It's like I'm tuned in to him, and I don't want to be.

He sits one seat behind and across one row. I don't think I've ever seen him sit that close to the teacher before. He usually sits in the back.

A low hum echoes through the hall and I take my notes out, ignoring everyone around me, including Karen. There's nothing like a bit of last-minute revision right before an exam. I think I'm good for this one though, like I have been for all the others.

When I finally do glance over my shoulder, Levi is staring at me with a frown on his face, and I quickly look away. Even with his forehead scrunched between his eyes, he's still so hot.

I do not need this distraction right now.

A piece of screwed up paper hits me in the back of the head, and I hear Veronica snigger. What I wouldn't give to have her disappear out of my life. I ignore her attempt to get my attention.

"All right, class. Settle down." Mr Jenkins shuffles the pile of test papers in his hands. "I trust you've all studied hard." He walks up and down the aisles, placing a test paper on each student's desk, face down. "You have two hours. No talking during this exam. And no cheating on your phones. Don't think I can't see you, Miss Porter." He looks down his nose at Veronica, then sits at the desk at the front of the hall. He looks at his watch. "You may start in three ... two ... one."

The room fills with the sound of rustling paper.

Something

The exam is okay, and I feel pretty confident that I'll do well. When I sit back in my seat and look around, pretty much everyone still has their heads down. Even Mr Jenkins is staring at his desk. I turn to risk a glance at Levi, and he looks up, his mouth set in a firm line. I quickly face the front of the room again.

Moments later, another piece of screwed up paper lands on my desk. My breath catches in my throat. What if Mr Jenkins sees? I could get in big trouble and be accused of cheating. When the teacher doesn't look up from his desk I exhale slowly and flatten out the note.

It doesn't say much, but I'm angry Levi would risk getting caught for something so stupid. I want to yell at him, but I can't do that in the middle of an exam.

The note reads: *What are you going to tell her?*

I risk another glance at Levi, chewing my bottom lip until I taste blood, and frowning at him. He looks back to his test. Neatly, underneath his messy handwriting, I tell him what I would have said if I could open my mouth.

You're an idiot.

I drop my hand to my side and line my throw up with the space at Levi's feet. I flick my wrist and hope the piece of paper lands in the right place. A minute later it's back on my desk.

I un-crumple it and stare at the piece of flattened paper in front of me.

The suspense is killing me.

Levi's reply makes me smile, because I can imagine the playful tone in his voice. I pick up my pen and write back to him.

You're still an idiot.

When I look up, Mr Jenkins regards me with a stern expression. "Your time is up. Pens down please."

I fold the paper into my palm, praying he hasn't seen it. Mr Jenkins walks the room, like he did at the start of the exam, to collect our papers. He reaches my desk, and I hold out my test so he can take it.

"Miss Sullivan, may I have the note as well, please?"

I stiffen in my seat, and a million thoughts run through my head. My first instinct is to lie, and deny having a note, but I'm not a liar. I have no choice but to give it to him.

"I'm sorry, sir."

My teacher takes the note and reads it, then looks around the room at every student in turn, paying close attention to those sitting near me. Karen is staring at me with her mouth open.

"Who else wrote this?" Mr Jenkins holds up the piece of paper. "This kind of behaviour will not be tolerated, especially during a trial HSC exam. Katie, go and see Mrs Pritchard immediately."

My cheeks flame with heat. I've never been sent to the headmistress's office before. I've never so much as been in trouble for anything at school before.

My teacher strides to the desk at the front of the hall, dumps the pile of exam papers on it, and opens his folder. He fills out a slip of paper and comes to give it to me.

"But sir, I—"

"Save it for Mrs Pritchard, Katherine. And as for the rest of you ..." Mr Jenkins looks around the room again. "If the other culprit does not own up in the next two minutes, I will fail all of you."

I take the piece of paper from Mr Jenkins and stand,

adjusting my bag on my shoulder.

"That's not fair," Veronica says. "Why should we fail because of *her?*"

For once, I actually agree with her.

Levi sits hunched over, tapping his pen on the desk. He raises his head and his gaze locks onto mine. His mouth opens, and my eyes widen. I shake my head once, no. He can't own up. He's the school captain. He'll get crucified for passing a note in an exam.

"I did it," Karen says, and I spin in her direction. "Send me to the headmistress, too."

My mouth drops open and I go to say something, but Levi beats me to it.

"No, sir. It was me." He grabs the strap of his backpack and stands from his desk. "Karen has nothing to do with this."

The class lets out a collective gasp.

Veronica scowls, and her look cuts through me like a knife.

I glance from my best friend to Levi. I know it wasn't Karen, but I love her for wanting to help.

"Very well." Mr Jenkins looks down his nose at Levi before filling out another slip. He staples our note to it.

I adjust my glasses and wait for Mr Jenkins to hand the piece of paper to Levi.

We walk to Mrs Pritchard's office in silence, and I'm not sure if I'm angry or happy. I think I'm both. In reception, Levi and I hand our slips to Ms Smythe, the office lady. She offers us a weak smile before going through a door to the left where Mrs Pritchard's office is.

Ms Smythe comes back to the counter. "Off you go."

She nods at the headmistress's door.

Levi goes first, and I follow him in. Mrs Pritchard takes her glasses off and sits back in her chair.

"To what honour do I owe the school captain and our star pupil?" she says.

Levi and I both know she knows why we're here. We say nothing.

"Sit." Mrs Pritchard points to the chairs that face her desk. "Passing notes in an exam—I have to say, I'm very disappointed."

"It's not Katie's fault," Levi says.

Mrs Pritchard clasps her hands together on the desk and leans forward. "Ah, but she participated. If she hadn't done so, Katie wouldn't be here."

"Are you going to fail us?" I ask.

Our headmistress looks at Levi and me in turn. "No. It's obvious what you were talking about had nothing to do with History."

I let out a long breath. "Thank you."

"However ... you both acted inappropriately, so you will both lose five marks from your score on the exam you just took."

Lose marks? I close my eyes for a second. This isn't good. What if my mark isn't high enough to cope with the loss? This could ruin my chance at dux.

"Can I ask you to go a bit easier on Katie, please?" Levi says. "I passed the note first. I should receive more punishment."

"You definitely haven't set a very good example in this instance, Levi. I should strip you of your position. However, I would like to believe that this boils down to an error in judgement rather than an attempt at cheating." Mrs Pritchard looks between us again. "But Katie will receive the same punishment. I hope your efforts have been worth it."

Heat rises into my cheeks and I look at my hands.

"Okay, thank you," Levi says.

"Dismissed." Mrs Pritchard picks up her glasses and puts them back on.

Levi stands and touches me on the shoulder. I follow him out of the office, and we make our way across the yard towards the back driveway. Trial exams are over, so we're free to go for the day, and it seems like most of the year twelves already have.

When we reach the back gate, Karen is waiting for me on one side, and Veronica and Jarred are waiting for Levi on the other. Veronica is sitting up on the brick wall that encloses the school grounds. If I had a knife I could carve the tension in the air. Veronica and Karen glare at each other, and I wonder what we've missed.

I raise my eyebrows at Karen. "What's going on?"

"Nothing," she says. "What the hell happened to you two?"

"We lost marks," I say.

"Five each. Off our score for that exam," Levi adds.

"And you're okay with losing marks?" Karen stares at me.

"Not exactly." I glance at Levi, and adjust my bag on my shoulder.

"Great. Love you and leave you then," Karen says to Levi. "Let's go, Katie."

"Not so fast." Veronica jumps down from the wall and

walks towards me. "You owe me an answer."

I take a deep breath. "Yes, I do. But I get to go next."

"Yes," Karen says, pointing a finger at Veronica. "She gets to go next."

"Of course. That's how the game works." Veronica crosses her arms. "What's it gonna be?"

I lick my lips and glance at Levi before looking Veronica straight in the eyes. "Dare."

She laughs. "Oh, this will be so much fun."

I smile. "Bring it, bitch."

7

Now it's my turn

Mum watches me push peas around my plate. Dad has his eyes trained on his food. I've already had the lecture, and I've wracked my brain for a way to figure out how to tell Mum and Dad I want to go out tonight. Usually getting in trouble at school means not going out and having fun five minutes later.

Veronica hadn't dared me to do anything straight away. Instead, she'd invited me to a party. Apparently it's an end-of-trial-exams celebration, but I'm not sure if it was pre-planned or if she just made it up on the spot. I would've thought I'd have heard about a party over the past two weeks.

The last thing I want to do is go, but I can't back out of this one, and Levi is picking me up at eight. Now would be a good time to get grounded.

Mum sets her fork down. "Really, Katie? The head-mistress?"

"I told you, it's not that big a deal."

"You do realise which house you're in?" Daniel asks between mouthfuls.

Dad remains silent, eating his dinner slowly and sipping his wine. His silence is worse than Mum's look of disappointment.

"We passed a note," I say. "It's not the end of the world. And we didn't cheat."

"You don't pass notes in an exam." Mum picks up her fork again and stabs her steak. "Losing marks could affect your chances at dux. And you need the best grade possible to get into a degree in law or medicine."

"Have you decided what you'd like to do yet?" Dad asks.

I shrug. "Not yet." *I want to do a fine arts degree.*

"Well, just don't do it again, okay, honey?" Dad pats my arm.

Daniel shakes his head. "If it were me, I'd be grounded for a month."

"What's the point in grounding her? She doesn't go anywhere," Mum says.

"I do so … sometimes."

"Sweetie, I'm teasing you." Mum smiles. "Finish your dinner."

"Actually, I want to go somewhere tonight." I look from Mum to Dad and back again. "One of the girls at school is having a party to celebrate the end of trials."

"Where is this party?" Dad asks.

"It's at Veronica's. You remember Veronica? Levi is

going to drive us." I pull my phone from my pocket to check the time. "We're supposed to be leaving in about an hour."

Mum frowns. "Okay. But be home by one o'clock. No later."

"What?" Daniel says. "You're letting her go?"

"Yes." Mum glances at him. "Katie can go."

"So unfair," Daniel mutters into his plate.

I actually agree with him.

We finish dinner in silence. Daniel and I clean up while Mum and Dad go out to the lounge room. I stack the dishwasher and wipe the benches while Daniel washes the frypan. He keeps looking at me from the corner of his eye.

"What?" I ask.

He flicks soap suds at me. "Can't believe they're letting you go out after stuffing up like this."

I shrug. "I have an untarnished record. Or at least I did."

Daniel chuckles. "So, Levi. Still just friends?"

"Yep." I concentrate on moving the sponge in circles across the bench.

"The guy you've been in love with for like, forever."

"I'm not in love with him." I grab Mum's pen off the counter and chuck it at him. "Next time, I will stab you."

"Katie, it's okay to like him." Daniel puts the frypan on the sink to drain.

I laugh. "No, it isn't. Girls like me should not have the hots for guys like Levi."

"Everything okay at school?" He leans against the bench and dries his hands on a tea towel. I chew the side of my thumb. "I'll take that as a no."

"I can take care of myself." I punch him on the arm. "Don't worry, I'm fine."

Daniel wraps me in a brotherly hug, resting his chin on the top of my head. "If you say so. But let me know if you need anything, okay?"

"I need to get ready. You can let go of me now." I pull away from my brother and head out of the kitchen.

"Katie," Daniel says, and I turn in the doorway. He presses his lips together. "Be careful. Okay?"

I nod. "Stop worrying. I'm fine."

I take the stairs two at a time and go to my room, closing the door. It's been a long day, and my mind is so full I feel like it's about to explode. I grab my journal off my desk and sit on the edge of my bed. Maybe if I get some stuff out, I'll feel a bit better.

It's truth-or-dare time tonight and I'm nervous. I've tried not to think about it too much. I've chosen dare, and I'm totally freaking out. What will Veronica ask me to do? And what will happen once it's my turn? Who will I truth or dare, and what will I ask them?

I don't know any dirty secrets about anyone, so my question would be lame. And I can't think of anything to dare anyone that they probably haven't been dared before. Do I have it in me to make someone do something awful? Has this whole thing turned me into a horrible person? I hope not. Besides, the only person I would really consider doing something mean to would be Veronica, but even so, I don't want to hurt her.

Levi is probably my safest bet. If he chooses dare, I can just think of something on the spot. Something lame to get it over with. But if he chooses truth, maybe I can ask him a question where the answer will tell me if he actually cares, or if it's all a show.

There's a tap at the window. A second later the bottom sash slides up and Levi sticks a leg through onto the window seat.

"What are you doing?" I ask, closing my journal and putting it back on my desk. "It's not time to go yet."

"No," he says, plonking onto the seat. "But this is your twenty-minute call. And I came to see if you wanted any help getting ready."

I raise my eyebrows but don't reply. My wardrobe doors are open, so I go stand in front of them and stare at my meagre fashion range. What am I supposed to wear to a party at Veronica Porter's house? She lives in one of the richest suburbs on the North Shore, so I'm not sure jeans and a jacket will cut it.

The hangers click as I search for something that doesn't say 'poor Katie', but I have nothing. I drop my hands to my side and sigh.

"Jeans will be fine," Levi says.

I look him up and down. He's wearing dark blue jeans, an ice-blue T-shirt, and a black leather flying jacket. He comes to the wardrobe and looks in, taking a pair of my jeans out and handing them to me. He rifles through the hangers and takes out a cream three-quarter-sleeved top with navy stripes. Then he grabs my grey chunky-knit cardigan. It's probably the nicest piece of clothing I own.

I screw my nose up. "That top doesn't really go with that cardigan."

Levi raises his eyebrows. "Why?"

"I wear white or black with grey. Not cream and navy."

He hands me the cardigan and puts the top back, choosing another simple black one. "This do?"

"Perfect," I say. "Now can you leave so I can get ready? And can you use the front door like a normal person?"

"Fifteen minutes?" He climbs out the window.

"I'll do my best."

I watch as Levi makes his way down the trellis. When he reaches the ground, I shut the window and pull my curtains closed. I'm not much of a makeup kind of girl, so it doesn't take me long to get changed and ready. I fluff my hair and leave it loose around my shoulders, then apply some gloss to my lips. I pull my only pair of heels from the back of the closet—short black leather boots with a suede section that slouches around my ankles, and buttons up the sides. I don't wear them much because I find high heels hard to walk in, so they look almost new.

I grab my favourite clutch purse, shoving my gloss, house keys, and phone inside on the way out of my room. A knock sounds at the front door as I'm walking down the stairs.

Mum answers it before I reach the bottom.

"Hi, Sonja," Levi says.

"Levi, how nice to see you." Mum opens the door wide.

Dad and Daniel appear from the lounge room.

I stop at the bottom of the steps and take a deep breath. This is the first time I've ever been right where I am now—with a gorgeous guy standing on my doorstep waiting to take me somewhere. I want to pinch myself, and then I remember where we're going and who else is going to be there. I take another deep breath.

Levi smiles at me. "You look nice. Ready?"

"Sure." I nod, my cheeks turning hot.

Dad steps forward and looks at Levi. "I trust you won't be drinking tonight?"

My stomach clenches and I bite my lip. Of all the questions he had to ask, it was the drinking one. I feel like yelling at him. Does he think Levi is that stupid? After what happened to his brother?

"No, of course not," Levi says. "Just a few of us watching a movie and having pizza to celebrate the end of trials." Levi smiles.

Daniel crosses his arms over his chest, and I think I'm going to pass out from all the deep breaths I'm taking.

"I'll be home by curfew." I move to the door and stand between Levi and my family.

Dad opens his mouth to say something, but Mum gives him a look. "Have fun," she says. "Call us if you need anything."

I gently push Levi off the threshold so we can get out of here, and close the door. Once it's shut behind us I look at him and laugh. "Sorry about that."

"S'okay." He shrugs. "They care about you."

We walk across our boundary, stepping through the garden bed to Levi's car, which is parked in his driveway.

The night air is chilly, and I rub my arms. He opens the passenger door for me and I slide in, pulling my cardigan tight around me. Levi gets in and starts the car. The BMW's engine rumbles to life. I fidget with my sleeve as we drive to Karen's place, nervous about what's going to happen tonight. I'm so glad she's coming with us. I don't think I would be able to do this on my own.

Karen is waiting in her driveway, and she has the back door open before Levi even comes to a full stop.

"Hey," she says as she climbs in, slamming the door.

I turn to look at her and smile, even though I feel so sick I think I might vomit.

"You look good, Karen," Levi says.

She blinks a few times. "What do you want?"

He chuckles. "Can't I give you a compliment?"

Karen sits back and fastens her seatbelt. "Didn't think you did compliments anymore."

"Maybe I'm turning over a new leaf." He glances sideways at me before he reverses back onto the street and takes off towards the highway.

I'm not sure what to make of his comment. There are so many things I'm confused about at the moment. What if his intentions aren't what I'm reading them to be? What if I think we have something, but we really don't? The thought makes my stomach twist into more knots, and by the time we reach Veronica's house, I really do think I'm going to be sick.

Levi parks on the street across the road from Veronica's. Cars line both sides of the road. When Levi told my parents 'just a few of us' were going to this party, I assumed he meant maybe ten people. The sounds coming from inside the house suggest a lot more than that. Like the whole of year twelve.

Karen gets out of the car, and I stare at her through my window. The lights from Veronica's place shine into the darkness. About five people are outside on the veranda that runs the length of the front of the house. More bodies move around inside, visible through the huge glass windows. Music pumps into the night, and I wonder what the hell I'm getting myself into.

Karen opens my door. Levi is beside her, looking down at me.

"You okay?" he asks.

No, I'm not okay. I don't want to move. "Sure." I smile up at him. "Looks like fun." *Looks like hell more like it.*

I swing my legs around and get out of the car, slipping my hand through the strap on my purse and clutching it to my chest. Karen pushes my door closed and links her arm through mine. The BMW's lights blink, and it beeps when Levi presses the button in his hand. I scan the street. Maybe I can make a getaway now.

"How the hell are we going to survive this?" I whisper to Karen.

"We'll be fine." She tugs me across the street and Levi follows. "We're better than every single one of these snobs."

I want to believe her, but I don't.

The three of us walk up the driveway towards the huge house. I recognise the people on the porch as kids from school, but I'm not friends with any of them. They stop talking and watch as Levi takes my hand and walks through the front door. I don't let go of Karen, so I'm sandwiched between my best friend and my ex best friend.

The lounge room on our left is crowded, with people sitting on every seat available, and others dancing to the music coming from the iPod dock in the corner. Levi keeps walking and takes us through into a gourmet kitchen, big enough to host a dinner party of twenty at the long timber table. We keep going through a set of double French doors and out to the backyard.

There aren't as many people here, and I take a big gulp of fresh air.

"Where are Veronica's parents?" I ask.

Levi lets go of my hand. "They'll be upstairs in their room. They let her have parties all the time. Although this is bigger than usual."

"Of course it is."

I glance around at the expansive yard. There's a recently mowed lawn leading to a swimming pool, then a tennis court up the back. The banana lounges are occupied, some of them with more than one person. I know everyone here by first name at least, but I wouldn't call most of them friends.

Over to one side is a big outdoor setting, and I spot Jessica sitting at the table with her sister, Josephine, and Jarred, Veronica, Geoff, and a few others. My gaze meets Veronica's, and she smirks. I catch Jessica's eye, but she's not smiling like Veronica is. I pull my arm from Karen's, even though I could use the support, because I don't want to look like I'm clinging onto her for dear life.

"Katie," Veronica calls. "So glad you could make it." She jumps up from her chair. "Now that you're here we can all go inside."

My stomach flips at the way Veronica is looking at me. I glance around the backyard. I'd much rather be outside in the open air, but everyone gets up, one by one, and follows Veronica towards the house.

"Be careful, Katie," Jessica says when she reaches me. "I don't know what she's got planned for you, but I think she's told some of the others."

"Don't worry," Karen says. "Veronica thinks she's smart, but she's got nothing on Katie."

I hope Karen is right. Veronica will either outsmart me and I'll get crucified in front of the entire year, or I'll get one over her and give her a very good reason to hate me even more.

"Just … be prepared," Jessica says.

"How the hell do I do that?" I ask.

Jessica shrugs.

Levi looks at me. "You okay?"

"Sure." I wish he'd stop asking me that because no. I'm nervous as all hell. I try to smile.

"Just remember what I told you." He grabs my hand and pulls me towards the house.

"This is not going to end well." Jessica rubs her arms, warding off the cool air.

"That's the spirit, Jess," Karen says.

I let out a half-laugh. "She's going to crucify me."

"I won't let that happen." Levi lets go of my hand when we reach the French doors at the back of the house.

We make our way into the kitchen. With a deep breath I grab a bottle of water from the stash on the bench, cracking the lid to take a sip. I pause in the doorway to the huge lounge room at the front of the house. The music has been turned down, and no one is dancing anymore.

I have a pretty big audience.

There are three three-seater lounges arranged in a U-shape around an open fireplace. I'm glad it isn't lit. If it were, I'd be sweating more than I already am from nerves. In front of the fireplace is a coffee table filled with cups, glasses, and bottles of alcohol. At least half the kids here are eighteen, so can legally drink, but there are a few with cups in their hands who I know are underage, and I bet they're not drinking water like me.

"I saved you a seat." Veronica points to the couch cushion beside her. She's sitting up on the arm with her feet on the lounge.

I stand tall and face her, promising myself that whatever she throws at me I'll be able to handle just fine. And then, I'll throw it back at her like a force-ten hurricane. She'll never know what hit her.

I make my way over, set my bottle of water on the coffee table beside a bottle of lethal-looking spirits, and sit down. Karen and Jessica follow, taking up positions on the floor near my feet. Karen leans against the big arm of the couch, and Jessica crosses her legs. Levi hangs back at the doorway, a drink in his hand.

The room buzzes with low conversation, and I stare at the carpet in front of me. I don't want to look around at everyone. I'm already nervous. Why the hell did I choose dare? I must be an idiot.

Karen slips her arm behind my leg and hugs it, resting her shoulder against my knee. I'm so glad she's here. At least I have her and Jessica on my side.

"Is everyone ready to play?" Veronica asks.

The room erupts with cheers.

"The real party starts now," someone yells, and a few people laugh.

"Remember the rules," Karen says. "Katie gets to go next."

"I wouldn't dream of breaking the rules," Veronica says.

Something

"Come on," I say. "What's my dare?"

"Okay, Katie." Veronica looks down at me from her perch on the arm of the lounge. "I dare you to drink five shots."

More cheers erupt around the room.

Five shots? Is she crazy? I'll fall into a coma.

Karen stiffens beside me. "Are you trying to kill her?"

"Just trying to have fun." Veronica smirks again and takes a sip from her cup.

I stare at the table, and that's when I notice the shot glasses already lined up in front of several different bottles of booze.

"You can pick your poison," Jarred says.

"Five shots of anything on this table." Veronica looks at me with a smirk.

Behind the five shot glasses are bottles of bourbon, vodka, rum, and scotch. Any one of those is going to have me flat on my back seconds after the fifth shot hits my stomach, if not before.

"Okay." I scoot forward to the edge of my seat.

I take a deep breath and let it out slowly. There has to be a way around this. I kneel then shuffle the two steps to the edge of the coffee table. The room has gone silent, and I stare at each bottle in turn, trying to decide which will do the least damage. I really have no idea though. I don't drink, and I've certainly never been drunk before.

Levi drinks bourbon, so maybe it's not that bad.

I pick up the bottle of Jim Beam and pour the first shot. I reach for the small glass of amber liquid, and cheers erupt around the room. Before I can chicken out, I bring the drink to my lips and tip my head back. The bourbon burns my throat on the way down, and I grimace.

"Blerk," I say. "That's horrible."

Laughter rolls around the room in waves.

"Four to go," Veronica says.

I find Levi and lock gazes with him. He's smiling, but it's not touching his eyes.

I lick my lips and pour another shot. My belly is warm from the first one, and now that the burning in my throat has gone, I feel kind of good. Maybe I'll come out of this okay. I throw back the second shot to more cheers and laughter.

My head spins a little as I pick up the bourbon bottle.

Or maybe I'm about to end up in the hospital. *Come on, Katie, don't let them beat you.* I lick my lips again and lean on the coffee table. My elbow brushes my bottle of water, and through the slight fuzz in my head I remember what Levi told me. There's always a way around a dare. You just have to find it.

I stare at my water for a few seconds, then put the bourbon bottle down beside it. I pick up the water and take the cap off.

"What are you doing?" Veronica jumps up.

I pour water into the three remaining shot glasses. "You said anything on this table."

"I didn't put that there." She glares at me.

I throw back the three shots of water. "But it was there when you told me the rules. Now it's my turn."

8

As it falls back into place

The room erupts with shouting. It's so loud I can't make out any words. Veronica's mouth drops open, and she stares at me.

"You can't do that." Rachel gets up from her seat on the couch opposite us. "That's cheating."

"Cheater, cheater, cheater," everyone in the room chants.

"No, it isn't." Karen gets to her feet. "You're all sore losers."

"Bitch," Veronica says.

I laugh and stand, swaying on my feet a little. "Is that your best comeback?" But my voice gets drowned out by the noise.

Veronica narrows her eyes and clenches her fists at her sides. Jessica stands, and I now have her on one side of me and Karen on the other. I follow Jessica's gaze around the room where it stops and rests on Josephine.

Jessica's sister shakes her head and rolls her eyes.

Levi jumps onto the coffee table, knocking over a few cups and a bottle of vodka. Thankfully, the lid is on.

"Stop!" he yells.

The room quietens to a murmur, and I look up at Levi. He glances down at me, a half-smile touching his lips. He goes to say something, but now that the noise has died down, Karen beats him to it.

"When are you going to get over the fact that Katie is smarter than you?" Karen's voice travels around the room. She folds her arms and glares at everyone.

Veronica takes a step towards me, but I stand my ground. Karen and Jessica do, too.

"You cheated," Veronica says, pointing a finger at me.

"Katie drank her shots." Levi jumps off the coffee table and lands in front of me. "It's her turn."

Veronica grits her teeth. "This better be good." She takes up her seat again on the arm of the couch.

Karen sits where I was, and Jessica squeezes in beside her, but I stay standing. I do not want to be sitting for this. In case I need to run away really quickly. Running away seems like a good idea, actually, because I don't want to do this.

"Levi, truth or dare?" The words are out of my mouth, and a second later I want them back.

The room erupts with chatter and cat-calling. Someone lets out an ear-piercing wolf whistle, and I cringe.

What the hell am I doing? What am I going to ask him if he says truth? What will I dare him if he doesn't? I thought maybe I was prepared for this, but it turns out I'm not. All eyes are on me, staring at the boy in front of me. The one I've been in love with my entire life. The one I have so many questions for, but they're ones I don't want to ask in front of a room full of rich-kid snobs.

I should never have come to this party.

Levi sits on the coffee table and stares up at me, that lopsided smile still playing on his face. He rests his hands on his knees and licks his lips.

"Truth," Levi says.

My mouth opens, and I close it again. Truth? *Shit!* What am I going to ask him that isn't too personal and won't reveal how much I like him? But I want to ask something that I get a decent answer for, otherwise this is all a waste of time and effort. Should I ask him something about his past? His brother?

No, that would be mean.

"What's your favourite childhood memory?" I blurt. *Lame.*

"Seriously?" Veronica says. "That's your question?"

Laughter erupts through the room.

Levi runs a hand through his hair and my knees go weak. He smiles wide, looking around at all the faces. "Come on, everyone. It's a good question."

I stand there and twist my hands together, unable to look at him, so I stare at my feet. My boots have a scuff mark on them and I make a mental note to polish them tomorrow.

"It's a sucky question," Rachel says.

"Why? Because it's not about sex?" Karen scowls at her.

"I have more than one," Levi says, "but do you remember the day Mason and I wanted to pull down the treehouse?"

I suck in a breath and look up, catching Levi's stare.

"Yes," I whisper.

"Mason thought we were all too old to have a treehouse. You got mad because it had taken us so long to build that thing. You didn't want us to pull it down, but I guess we were going through a destructive phase. If we could break it, we would."

A few chuckles roll around the room, and it seems like everyone is suddenly hanging onto every word Levi says.

"I told you we had to keep the purple flower curtains, because I'd made them myself." I smile. I have so many great memories of spending time in that treehouse.

"Yeah." Levi smiles back at me, and rubs his legs with his palms. "You also said if we tore it down, you'd never speak to either of us again. You were so angry, and I remember thinking, you're really pretty when you're angry." He stops and takes a breath.

I have the chance to say something, but I don't. Levi just admitted in front of everyone that he thought I was pretty. But we were only fourteen then. Does he still think the same now? The room is silent, and I wait for someone to say something, but no one does. My heart pounds, and I stare down at my twisted hands again.

"But my favourite part about that day happened later," Levi says.

"I bet you got some," Jarred yells, and I cringe.

"You and me in the treehouse, Katie. There's more than one memory that's my favourite."

"Woohoo," someone yells.

"It's always about sex," another voice calls out.

"You did it with *her*?" Veronica asks.

Levi doesn't say yes or no, and the room erupts again.

Something

I stare at Levi with my mouth open. What has he done? Here I was thinking I'd asked a simple, innocent question, and he's turned it into something where everyone thinks we were together.

He's made something from absolutely nothing.

There is nothing going on between us. As much as I've always wanted something with Levi, it's never happened.

"Is this some cruel joke?" I ask. "You want them to think we did it in the treehouse?"

But I don't wait for an answer. I do what I wanted to do the moment we first pulled up to Veronica's and I got out of Levi's car.

I run.

I run through the people clogging the lounge room and out onto the porch. I run down the driveway to the street.

I can't believe he's letting everyone think those things. I've never even kissed anyone, but I know exactly what they *are* thinking back in that house.

"Katie, wait," Levi calls, but I don't turn around.

I keep running.

The train station isn't far. I'll jump on the next train home and walk the half an hour to my house. Another set of footsteps sounds behind me. Levi grabs my arm and pulls me to a stop.

I reef myself from his grip. "Don't touch me!"

The streetlight casts a glow over his face. "Katie—"

"What the hell was that back there? We never did anything in that treehouse."

"I know we didn't."

"Then why did you let them believe we did?"

"Because I want everyone to know that I like you."

My breath catches in my throat. I stare at him and shake my head. "And this is the way you do it? You're an idiot!"

"Katie?" Karen yells.

She runs along the footpath, Jessica behind her.

"Over here." I step from the shadows, so she can see me in the streetlight.

Karen's feet pound the ground. "Get away from her, you arsehole." She stops between Levi and me, and I take a step back.

Jessica reaches us a few seconds later. "He's more than that! You're ... you're a dick, Levi. How dare you make everyone think you and Katie ..." She stops and puts her hands on her hips. I've never heard Jessica speak to anyone so meanly. She's usually so quiet, and always nice.

"We should never have come." I take Jessica's hand and pull her away from Levi. "I'm going home."

"If you want to go, I'll take you," Levi says.

"Like hell you will." Karen steps towards him.

"Okay." He raises his hands and backs away.

"I have Josie's car." Jessica pulls her phone from her pocket. "She can get a lift with *you*." She quickly types a text to her sister, then re-pockets her phone. "Come on."

Karen and I follow Jessica down the street, and I feel Levi's presence behind us. We find Josephine's Honda. Jessica pushes the button on the remote and the locks pop. I go to open the passenger door, but Levi beats me to it.

"Would you go away?" I say. "I'm really angry at you."

"Doesn't mean I can't be nice." He smiles, and it's so infuriating.

Something

"Go away, Levi." Karen gets in the back, slamming her door.

Jessica sits behind the wheel and starts the engine.

I climb into the car, rest my purse in my lap, and pull my cardigan tight around myself, refusing to look at Levi. Here I was worried about falling on my face because of Veronica's dare, and instead I've been humiliated because of a stupid question *I* asked. One Levi answered truthfully. But which also suggested I'd slept with him when we were fourteen. How could he embarrass me like that?

I grab the door and pull it out of Levi's grip, slamming it. Jessica drives towards the motorway and I rest my head against the seat, closing my eyes. A tear slips out and I quickly wipe it away. I'm not going to be the girl who cries over something a guy she likes did. I stare out the window and watch the lights of the oncoming traffic.

Jessica takes our exit and turns onto the highway, making the next left to head towards Karen's house. We pull up in her driveway, and Jessica kills the engine.

Karen unbuckles her seatbelt and leans forward between the front seats. "You gonna be okay?"

I roll my head to the side and look at my friends. "Aren't I always?"

"Call me if you need me." Karen kisses me on the top of the head, then gets out of the car.

Jessica and I watch her until she's inside, then we reverse out of the driveway and head for home. She pulls up to the kerb outside my house, and I open my door and get out.

"Thanks, Jess," I say through the open door.

"Don't worry about what they all think," she says.

"You know the truth. That's all that matters."

I sigh and sit back on the edge of the car seat. "I'm so mad at him, but it's weird, because I'm also excited about what he said. He basically told everyone he thinks I'm pretty. That's good, right?" I look at Jessica.

She reaches over and takes my hand. "You and Levi … it would be awesome. I always used to think you'd end up together. But just … be careful. The way they play truth or dare isn't always fun."

I press my lips together. "Yeah."

Jessica squeezes my hand and I get out of the car again, closing the door. She gives me a wave and drives the few houses down the street to her place. I watch until she turns into her driveway, and then I walk down mine to the front door.

Mum and Dad are on the couch watching a movie.

"Katie," Mum says. "Everything okay? We weren't expecting you home yet."

"Yeah, I'm fine. Tired." I close the front door. "I'm going to bed."

Dad frowns. "Sure you're all right?"

"All good." I kick my boots off and go upstairs.

When I close my door, I suck in a deep breath and throw my purse on my desk. I'm not sure what to do with myself, or how to feel, so I stand in the middle of my room for a minute and close my eyes. How did I get here? What did I ever do to deserve people treating me the way they do?

I'm not a bad person. I've never intentionally hurt anyone. And I'm so sick of not being good enough. I can't wait for this year to be over so I can be rid of that stupid private school and all its ugliness.

I take my cardigan off and hang it back in my wardrobe, then I change into my flannelette PJs and flop onto my bed.

My phone buzzes with a message.

Karen: U OK?

Me: Will liv

Karen: Call me 2morrow

Me: xxx

I toss my phone back onto my desk and fall onto my pillow. I don't want to go to bed yet. I'm not actually tired, but what else am I supposed to do? Exams finished today so the last thing I need to do is study. I can have at least one day off.

I grab my journal and bunny and take them over to the window seat. After settling onto the cushion, I drape my crochet blanket over my knees and open my journal to the next blank page.

Tonight was a disaster. What the hell was I thinking, getting involved with Veronica and her friends? I should never have truth or dared Levi. I should've picked Karen. Looking at it now, why didn't I take that easy choice? She would've done anything I asked her to, or answered any question, and made everyone laugh in the process.

I'm an idiot.

All I've done is given everyone something to talk about. And I'm so angry at Levi for the way he answered my question. But I also love that he called me pretty. It's so confusing. Why do boys always have to show off like that to their friends? Making everyone think I slept with him. I wanted to slap him, and I hate that he brings out these

feelings in me.
Why can't it be easier?

A few hours later, a car rumbling outside pulls me from my thoughts and I close my journal. I part the curtains and stare down at Levi's driveway. The lights of his BMW flick off and the driver's side door opens, but Levi doesn't get out. Instead, Josephine steps onto the concrete.

Levi must have had too much to drink—again.

Josephine closes her door and goes around the front of the car to the passenger side. She almost gets hit in the face when Levi throws his door open. He stumbles out and she tries to catch him, but they fall onto the grass together. Josephine giggles and leans in close to whisper something in Levi's ear.

He glances up at my window, and I quickly close the curtains.

I hear the car door slam. Josephine giggles again, and I can only imagine what they're doing. The last thing I should do is look. What if I see something I don't want to see? But I can't help it, and I part the curtains again.

Josephine hangs off Levi's arm, and they walk to the street where they stop at the kerb. She stands on her tiptoes and slowly presses her mouth over his. I yank the curtains closed. What is going on? Why is he letting her kiss him when I thought he liked me? If this is part of Veronica's game to get to me, then it's worked.

I part the curtains again. Levi stands on the kerb, watching Josephine as she walks along our street. He runs his hand through his hair, and my heart breaks a little more.

Something

I let go of the curtains and get up, tossing my journal onto my desk. *Don't let it get to you.* I pace my room, angry because Levi made everyone think we'd been together when we hadn't, and he also told me I'm pretty, but then he went and flirted with Josephine. *I can't figure him out.*

I flick my hands as I pace, trying to get rid of the horrible feeling inside me. This all started at the beginning of term, when Levi decided to climb in my window drunk. I want to go back to that night so I can tell him I never want to see him or speak to him again, and then none of this would have happened. There would be nothing happening between us, instead of something that I have no control over, something I don't completely understand.

But is that what I actually want?

A part of me has always hoped Levi and I would have something one day.

A sound outside pulls me from my thoughts. The curtains part, and Levi sticks his head through the window. He pulls his knee up and climbs in, falling onto the window seat.

I stare at him, not sure if I want to yell or cry.

"My parents are home," I whisper.

Levi stares at me. His eyes have that glassy drunk look. "Then we better be quiet."

"How drunk are you?"

"I'm fine. Nothing like …"

"The time you climbed in here after face-planting the ground?"

"Nothing like that."

I climb into bed and pull the covers up to my waist,

propping my pillow against the bedhead and leaning back.

"You looked pretty drunk when Josephine helped you out of the car."

"You saw that?" Levi stares at his feet.

"She kissed you."

"I pushed her away."

The silence hangs between us for a moment.

"Really?" I finally ask.

"You didn't see me push her away?"

I shake my head.

Levi sighs, then looks at me. "I'm sorry, Katie."

"You know, after tonight, I don't really want to talk to you."

Levi moves to sit on the end of the bed and stares at his hands. His hair flops over his eyes, and I want to reach out and push it away, but I don't.

"I'm *really* sorry. Veronica, she ... I don't know." He sighs again.

"She's a bitch is what she is." My voice is almost a whisper.

Levi pushes his hair away from his eyes and sits up straighter. "She can be, but—"

"No!" I look directly at him. I'm not going to let him do this. "Don't you dare stick up for her. Don't make excuses for the way she treats me. Or the way *you* treat me."

"What ...?" Levi stares at me, his mouth slightly open.

I clutch the edge of my blankets. "You ... what you did tonight."

"I know. I realise how much of an arse I've been."

"Tonight? Or for like, forever?"

Levi shrugs. "Both. I shouldn't have let everyone think

that we … in the treehouse. I'm not proud of what I've done to you. What I've let others do to you. You were my best friend, and I threw you away like a piece of garbage."

I scoff. "Yeah, you did."

Levi moves up the bed so he's sitting closer to me. He reaches out and takes my glasses off, carefully closing the arms before laying them on my desk. I let my hair fall across my face. Not having my glasses on makes me feel exposed. They're like my security blanket.

"Don't." Levi puts his finger under my chin and raises my head. "I meant what I said tonight. I think you're pretty. You're beautiful, actually. Someone needs to tell you that more often."

I shake my head. "Me? No, I'm not … I'm nothing."

"That's not true." Levi studies me for a moment. "You're something, Katie. You're smart, and funny, and kind. You're the most beautiful person I know."

"Then why did you do what you did?" I tuck my hair behind my ear and pull away from him, looking at my hands. "Why did you … leave me?"

"I thought we'd worked this part out," he says, a joking tone in his voice. "I'm a jerk."

"I'm serious, Levi," I whisper. "Why?"

My eyes burn with hot tears, and I force myself to hold them back. I will not cry in front of Levi.

"Because … you're not like the other girls. You're not like any of my friends. You don't fit with them, and … I was ashamed to know you."

I squeeze my eyes closed and suppress a sob, but the tears still manage to find their way out and tumble down my cheeks. I blink them away. "I'm not rich like the rest of you, so you're ashamed of me?"

"I'm so sorry." Levi reaches out and wipes a tear from under my eye with his thumb. His hands are rough but somehow comforting. Still, I pull away. I swipe at my face, then grab my glasses from the desk and put them back on.

We sit in silence. I'm too afraid to speak because I don't think my voice will work properly. After a few minutes, Levi stands and goes to the window.

"Are you leaving?" I ask.

"You need some sleep. Can I see you tomorrow?"

I shrug. "I don't know."

"I want to see you."

"Well, I don't know what I want." And I don't. I'm so confused about everything. "I'm not sure I can trust you."

Levi comes back to the bed and leans down, kissing me on the forehead. "I hope you can again someday, because I've been an idiot, and I will do anything to make it up to you. I've been too blind to see that the one thing I've needed the most has been right in front of me all along."

He climbs out the window, and I stare at the curtain as it falls back into place.

9

Why is it so hard in the first place?

aturday, I don't go anywhere. I'm not really in a house-leaving kind of mood, so I stay in my room listening to music and writing in my journal. I fill ten pages, but stop after that because all I'm writing about is Levi and how I feel about everything that's happened. His apology hangs over me, and as much as I want to believe he was being genuine, I'm not sure if I should trust his words or prepare for the worst again.

Now, it's Sunday morning. Karen pulls into my driveway, and I race to the front door.

"Katie?" Mum calls. "Remember what I said."

"I know, Mum," I yell over my shoulder. *Spend the money wisely.*

I pull the passenger-side door open and climb into Karen's mum's car, shoving my tote and cardigan on the

floor at my feet.

"Ready to rock?" Karen asks.

"Yep. Let's hit the road."

Karen reverses out of the driveway and I glance over at Levi's house. He's standing on the front veranda leaning against the stair railing. He raises his hand and gives me a wave. I offer him a small smile, then look straight ahead. Even after pouring everything into my journal, I'm still not sure how I feel about our last conversation, and I'm not going to let anything ruin today, so thinking about Levi is off limits.

Karen and I head to the shops to look for our formal dresses, and this time we have to come home with something because graduation is only a month away. We wanted Jessica and Stacey to come, too, but they had other plans. I'm not that excited about going to the formal, but I'm looking forward to spending time with Karen, and using the small amount of money Mum and Dad gave me wisely.

After parking the car and grabbing a quick hot chocolate, we hit the shops.

"You would look hot in that dress," Karen says, stopping at a shop window and pointing to a sleek, black pencil number.

"Yeah, if I worked in an office and was ten years older. What is it with you and pencil dresses? Come on, Karen, it's not a formal dress."

"But you'd still look great in it. We should get you a few other things today." Karen grins and claps her hands. "Oh, this will be fun. We can give you a whole new look."

"What's wrong with my look?" I stop and stare at her.

Karen tilts her head to the side and studies me. "Let's

at least get your hair trimmed. We can talk about your glasses later." Karen grabs my hand and pulls me to the closest hair salon.

"I don't usually have my hair done here," I say.

"Which is why we're going to go here. Relax." Karen leads me through the door.

"I thought we were shopping."

"We have all day." Karen waves her hand at me. "This won't take too long."

"I don't want anything off the length." Despite the many things I don't like about myself, my hair isn't one of them.

"Trimmed, I said *trimmed*." Karen turns to the girl behind the counter. "And maybe some foils."

The girl has heavy eye makeup, and black hair with a purple streak. She takes me through the salon and seats me at the only free station. At least there are other people in here, so hopefully I won't end up looking like an apprentice's mistake. I don't like the thought of having someone other than my normal hairdresser touching my hair.

The girl walks away, and I whisper to Karen, "Please don't let her dye my hair black." I like my brown waves, even if brown is boring.

"Foils," Karen says. "Golden ones."

She has a discussion with the hairdresser as if I'm not here. They look at the colour book, and Karen shakes her head a few times. When they finally agree the girl shows me the little swatch of hair, which is a nice golden blonde. I'm nervous, though. I've never put any colour through my hair. What if it turns out to be a disaster?

Karen smiles, and I decide to trust her, so I sit back and let the girl work her hairdressing magic. She divides my hair into sections, putting in foils until my head is covered with little folded bits of silver.

"I'll leave you for thirty minutes to process." She smiles at me in the mirror. "Then we'll wash your hair and give it a tidy up." She goes to the front counter to process some other customers' payments, and then busies herself cleaning up.

I glance around at the other people in the salon. Everyone seems happy, and no one has walked out looking hideous.

"See?" Karen says. "You need to do something different once in a while."

"She hasn't washed it out yet," I say. "Don't speak too soon."

When I'm finally finished an hour and a half later, I can't believe what I see in the mirror. The hairdresser has woven beautiful golden highlights through my previously flat brown locks, and layered it slightly so it falls nicely around my face and over my shoulders.

I almost don't believe it's me staring out of the mirror.

"All done," the girl says. "Come to the counter when you're ready."

Karen grins as I run my fingers through my new hairstyle. Then something occurs to me.

"Um, how am I going to pay for this?" I look at Karen in the mirror. "Mum and Dad only gave me money for a dress."

"This one's on me." Karen walks to the front of the store, and I follow. She takes out two fifties and lays them on the counter. She gets a dollar change.

Something

"I can't let you do that," I say.

"Yes, you can. Come on, it's time to shop." Karen grabs my hand and pulls me out of the salon and into the shopping centre.

"You planned this, didn't you?" I ask as we walk, looking in shop windows.

"You're welcome." Karen slips her arm through mine.

We spend the next hour checking out the department stores. They don't have much in the way of formal dresses, but I end up buying a couple of cheap singlet tops and a nice sheer top to wear over them. I'm a little hesitant at first, but Karen talks me into it. The top is green with a paisley pattern and little cap sleeves. It flows nicely around my waist and will go perfectly with my favourite pair of jeans.

Karen plays with my hair at the checkout. "Wait till Levi sees you."

I take a deep breath. "He climbed in my window again after the party."

"What? And you're only telling me now?"

"It's not a big deal. He just wanted to apologise. I'm not sure how I feel about everything though. It's all so … hard."

"Love isn't meant to be easy." Karen squeezes my arm.

"Can we not talk about this now?"

Karen smiles. "Whatever you want."

We leave the store and head back into the main shopping centre. There are a few small dress shops we can look in, so we start with the closest one. I have trouble finding anything I like enough to try on, so for the next hour I sit in the change room vestibule while Karen tries on dress after dress.

She finally narrows it down to two, and stares at me impatiently as I look back and forth between the dresses she's holding up.

"I think we should try another store," I say.

"You don't like these?" She clutches the hangers to her chest.

"It's not that. Just … maybe there are nicer ones in another store. And red … it's a bit much.

"It's the formal. We're supposed to stand out."

"I don't want to stand out."

"Maybe red is a bit much." Karen goes back into the change room.

"Try the blue one on again," I say. "I like it better than the red. The fabric is really nice."

"Okay." She rustles around in the change room, then opens the door.

I nod. "Yep. I like it. More now that I've seen it on you again."

Karen walks into the vestibule and twirls, looking in the full-length mirror.

The sales lady comes in. "Slip your feet into these." She grabs a pair of black heels from the floor and hands them to Karen. "You can get a better idea of what it will look like with shoes."

"Thanks." Karen slips them on.

"I take it you have a formal coming up?" the sales lady says.

We both nod.

"I think I'll take this one." Karen runs her palms over the fabric covering her stomach.

Something

The dress is really beautiful. It's ice blue and has a strapless sweetheart bodice with beading all over it. Then it gathers under the bust and falls in soft waves of chiffon to the floor. Karen looks at herself in the mirror for a few moments more, then gets changed. She pays for her dress, a smile plastered to her face.

We wander through the shops a bit, and every dress shop Karen suggests we go into I make an excuse not to enter. I'm just not a fancy-dress kind of girl, and I know what I'm looking for, but at the same time I don't. It's the kind of thing I have to see … and then I'll know.

We stop outside a small bohemian shop, and I grab Karen's arm. "I want to look in here."

"In the hippie shop?" Karen asks. "I don't think you'll find a formal dress in there."

"Can we just look?" I grab her hand and pull her into the store.

I do a lap of the shop, taking everything in first, then I search through a couple of racks up the front. One particular dress catches my eye. It's the kind of dress that's begging to be bought, even if I had nowhere to wear it, and I want it because it's so unusual. It's like someone took my personality and made it into a piece of clothing.

I take it from the rack and hold it up to get a better look. Biting my lip, I drape it in front of me and gaze down at the dress.

"That's gorgeous," Karen says.

"I know." I beam at her.

"You have to try it on."

"I know!" I almost squeal.

"The end change room is free," the sales lady says.

"It's a very lovely dress."

I smile and follow her to the small cubicles at the back of the store. Inside, I shimmy out of my jeans and top, then put the dress on. For a moment, all I can do is stare at my reflection. I'm pretty sure no one at the formal will have the same dress as me. None of those snobs would be seen dead wearing anything that's not covered with diamantes and made of silk or velvet, or whatever expensive fabric they think is on trend.

The dress is perfectly bohemian, and soft and feminine at the same time. It's strapless with a sweetheart neckline and ruched multi-coloured fabric in purples, pinks, blues, and a little yellow. A wide embroidered band encircles my waist. The skirt flows in layers of fuchsia and dark purple which are shorter at the front and longer at the back. A large flower print runs randomly along the hem to complete the look.

Wearing this dress makes me feel amazing.

I step out of the change room and Karen's mouth drops open.

"Oh. My. God!" She jumps up and down and squeals. "That is ... wow. You look ... I think I'm tearing up." She mock-wipes her eyes and I laugh.

"Isn't it beautiful?" I twirl and Karen squeals again.

I change back into my regular clothes, and pay for the dress. As we leave the store, I smile so much it hurts because not only do I have an awesome dress, but I have enough money left over to find some matching shoes.

We jump on the travelator to head to the ground floor and the shoe shop.

"Well, look who's had her hair done." Veronica stands

at the bottom of the travelator with Rachel.

Britney comes out of the chemist. "You guys, I found the most amazing nail polish." She stops beside Veronica and looks up at Karen and me.

I want to turn and run back up the travelator.

The smart thing to do would be to get to the bottom and walk past all of them. But I guess I'm still mad after Friday night. I step off and walk right into Veronica because she's in the way.

She stumbles backwards. "What are you doing, skank?"

"You're in my way." I face her. "Did you expect me not to get off the travelator?"

"Don't think for one second anything real will happen between you and Levi." Veronica folds her arms and stands taller. "I've seen how you look at him. But he's way out of your league."

As much as I agree with her, I'm done with trying to be nice all the time, and I'm not going to let her talk to me like this anymore.

"Get lost, Veronica," I say. "You're nothing but a jealous bitch."

"Who do you think you are?" Rachel flicks her hair over her shoulder. "You can't talk to her like that."

Britney stays quiet.

"I can do whatever I want." I glare at the three of them.

Karen grabs my arm. "Come on, Katie. They're not worth the time."

We walk away, and I'm itching to look over my shoulder, or give Veronica the finger, but I don't want to give her the satisfaction. I ball my hands and cross my arms tightly over my chest, wishing Veronica didn't get under my skin so easily.

Karen and I head towards the shoe shop, even though more shopping is the last thing I feel like doing now. Karen must sense my mood plummet and she squeezes my arm.

"Shoes, and then we're gone. Okay?"

I nod. "Sounds like a plan."

"You won't need many accessories with that dress. It speaks for itself."

I smile and we enter the shop, confronted by rows and rows of shoes. I walk down the aisle where the size sevens are, and browse what's on offer. There isn't much to choose from and I drag Karen back out of the shop five minutes later.

"Let's go up to the department store. They might have something on sale," I say.

We make our way upstairs again, this time using the steps instead of the travelator, and wander through the department store to the shoe section. Karen goes straight for the glitzy heels lining the wall, while I take a look at the sale tables. My hopes of finding something aren't great, but I spot one shoe from an unusual pair of wedges tucked under a hot pink flat.

The shoe has a decent platform, which will be great to give me some height, but it's the black lace that I love. They're peep-toes, with a T that goes up the front of the foot to a wide ankle band and a zipper at the back. I check the size. Seven and a half. I groan. They probably won't fit. I want to try them anyway, so I take the shoe over to the counter to ask the sales lady for the other one.

"Oh, they're really cool," Karen says. "Beautiful but

not flashy, so they won't take away from the dress."

"Let's hope they fit," I say. "I'm a seven and I think they're the last pair."

"I'll check if we have your size," the sales lady says, going through a doorway into the store room. She comes back a few minutes later with a box and the other shoe to the pair. "All I have left are the seven and a half, and a size nine."

"May as well try it," Karen says with a shrug.

"These are a smaller make, so you might find they'll fit." The sales lady smiles.

I sit in one of the courtesy chairs and kick off my Converse. The sales lady undoes the zipper and hands me the first shoe. *Please fit.* I've never wanted shoes to fit so badly before. *What is wrong with me?* I slip one on, then the other, and stand, the zippers still undone.

"They look awesome," Karen says.

"I think they'll be okay." I look down at my feet encased in the black lace wedges, and my mood lifts. Karen's right, shopping does fix everything.

Karen crouches and does the back zippers up. "Go for a walk."

The shoes are higher than anything I would usually wear, but they feel pretty sturdy on my feet. I think I'll be able to walk in them. I take a few steps, then stride the length of the shelving along the wall, turning at the end and walking back to the chair.

"You have to get them," Karen says. She has the box in her hands, staring at the price.

I smile so big my cheeks hurt, then sit and take the shoes off.

"I'll ring them up for you," the sales lady says.

After paying for the shoes, we decide we don't want to go home yet, so Karen and I grab a late lunch. Then we spend another few hours hanging out, looking at jewellery and window shopping. By five o'clock we've both had enough so we make our way back to the car.

Karen presses the button on her key ring and the door locks on the Swift pop open. I fall into the passenger seat, tossing my shopping bags at my feet.

"That was an awesome day." Karen starts the engine, then swings the car out of the car space and drives towards the exit. "Shopping, and standing up to Veronica."

"She'll pay me back on Monday." I rest my head against the seat.

"Don't worry. I've got your back." Karen turns onto the highway towards home.

We don't talk much during the twenty-minute drive, and when she pulls into my driveway I turn to her, trying to find the right words to thank her for everything, but I don't know what to say.

"I ... you ..." I tighten my grip on the handles of my shopping bags. "You're the—"

"Sweetie, you don't have to tell me." Karen smiles. "I know I'm awesome."

Laughter bubbles out of my mouth. "Yes, you are. And I love you so much for it."

"I'll always be here for you, no matter what."

What can I say to that? I hug her, then get out of the car and close the door. "Thanks," I say through the open window.

"No problem. And you know what?" Karen leans over

to look at me. "I think you need to ditch the glasses. It will totally complete the makeover. You have such pretty eyes."

"I don't know if I can do that."

"Sure you can."

"I've tried contacts before, and I hate sticking my finger in my eye."

"Promise me you'll try?" Karen grips the steering wheel, staring at me. "At least so you don't have to wear glasses to the formal."

"Okay." I nod.

"That's my girl."

I watch Karen drive away before turning towards the house.

Raised voices come from Levi's place and I stop to listen, but the words are muffled, and I can't make them out. I take a step and Levi bursts out the front door, his brow knitted and his face dark with anger.

"Get your arse back in here," Levi's dad yells from the open front door.

"Screw you." Levi stumbles towards me, blood trickling from a cut on his lip.

Mark glares at his son from the veranda before retreating inside and slamming the door.

"Levi, what happened?" I ask.

"Nothing I can't handle." He walks towards my front steps. When he reaches them, he sits down heavily and rests his head against the post.

I follow him. "Are you drunk? It's five thirty in the afternoon."

"I've been at Jarred's. Lunchtime party with the boys."

Like that explains everything.

I dump my shopping bags on the veranda and sit beside him. "Your lip is bleeding."

Levi faces me. "It's nothing."

"Do you want me to get a washcloth?"

He wipes his mouth with the back of his hand and looks at the red smudge on his skin. "Nah, it's fine."

"I'm going to get Mum." I stand, but Levi grabs my hand and pulls me back to the step.

"You've done something to your hair. It looks pretty."

Heat creeps into my cheeks, making them tingle, and I look away. "Karen took me shopping today ... It's nothing special."

"Don't do that, Katie." Levi lifts my chin with his finger. "The colour is really nice."

I push my glasses up my nose, and I wish I didn't have them on. Maybe Karen is right. Maybe I need to ditch them.

I reach up and touch Levi's lip. It looks like someone hit him. "What happened? Who ... Who hurt you? Is this why you drink?"

"Dad ... Mason ... Everything is easier to deal with through the haze."

Did his dad hit him? "It shouldn't be this way."

"A lot of things shouldn't be the way they are," Levi says.

"Will you be okay to go home?" I ask.

Levi licks his lips and nods. "I'll be fine."

"I'm really sorry. What can I do to help?"

"Nothing, Katie. I'll be fine."

The door behind us opens and Mum steps onto the veranda. "I thought I heard voices out here."

I grab my shopping bags and get to my feet. "We were

just talking."

Levi stands and jumps the steps to the path. "I'll see you tomorrow, Katie. Bye Sonja." He stuffs his hands into his pockets and walks back towards his house, stumbling once on the way.

"Come on, honey. Dinner's almost ready." Mum opens the door and we go inside. "Your hair looks great."

I smile and stop at the bottom of the stairs. "Thanks, Mum." I stare at her.

"Something up?" She raises her eyebrows.

"I'm worried about Levi. I think … he's having trouble at home."

I think his dad hit him.

"Did Levi tell you that?"

"Not exactly, but he came out of the house with Mark yelling at him. He had blood on his lip."

She purses her lips and squeezes my shoulder. "I'm sure they'll work it out."

I nod and go up to my room, hanging my dress on the wardrobe doorknob and setting the rest of my shopping bags on the bed. Maybe I'm wrong and Levi's dad didn't hit him. Maybe Levi got into a fight with one of his mates, or he walked into a door.

Who am I kidding? I decide to ask him the next time I see him.

I go to the bathroom, and while I'm washing my hands I study my new hair colour. I'm really happy with the result. I take my glasses off and splash some water on my face. After drying off, I go to put my glasses back on but stop. Karen said I should get rid of them, and Levi told me my eyes shouldn't be covered up.

I've tried contacts before, but I could never get used to sticking my finger in my eye. I have sensitive eyes so if I wore them I'd need to take them out every day. It seems like more hassle than it's worth, but maybe I should try again. And if I want to wear them to the formal, I need to get used to them now.

There are some disposables in the top drawer where I left them when I gave up the first time. I check the packet and they're still in date, so I decide that since I have new hair, I'll give them another go tomorrow.

Back in my room, I stand and stare at my new dress.

Daniel walks past, then stops and rests his hand against the doorjamb.

"You bought a dress."

I nod. "You make it sound like a crime."

"No, it's just ... you. Bought a dress." He scratches his head. "I didn't think you wanted to go to the formal."

"I don't really." I sit on the edge of my bed and press my hands between my knees. "Karen convinced me. And I saw this ..." I shrug.

"It's nice," Daniel says. "Very you." He comes into the room and sits next to me. "Everything okay?"

"You don't have to do the concerned big brother thing," I say. "I'm fine."

"How're things with Levi?"

I chew the side of my thumb and stare at the carpet. "There is no *thing* with Levi."

Daniel sighs and drapes his arm around my shoulders. "It gets easier."

"Why is it so hard in the first place?"

The fairy-tale ending I've always wanted

Going to school today is not at the top of my want-to-do list, especially after the party at Veronica's on Friday night, and running into her on the weekend. But I guess I have to get back into the swing of things. Now that trials are over, the HSC exams are a little more than a month away.

I'm hoping my new hair will draw attention away from what happened at the party.

Who am I kidding? A cut and colour aren't going to save me.

It takes me half an hour to get the contacts in my eyes. I lean over the basin in the bathroom as a wave of nausea crashes over me. The main reason I gave up the first time hits me right in the guts. Still, I'm determined to get used to them. No four-eyes photos for me at the formal.

As I walk into the kitchen, Dad looks up from his morning paper "Your hair is lovely. Did you use the money we gave you?"

I shake my head and sit across from him at the table. "Karen gifted it to me. I couldn't say no. She practically dragged me into the salon and tied me to the chair."

"Well, it really suits you." Mum grabs a piece of toast that's popped from the toaster.

"Where are your glasses?" Dad asks.

"Contacts," I say.

"She spent half an hour getting them in." Mum sets a cup of coffee in front of Dad.

Dad readjusts his paper. "Who are we impressing at school today?"

I say "no one" at the same time Daniel comes into the kitchen and says "Levi".

"Karen said I needed a change." I scowl at my brother.

"It's a nice change." Mum hands me a plate with honey toast on it.

"Need a lift today?" Daniel asks.

I grab my toast and put the plate in the sink. "Nah. I'll bus it with Jess. I've left her on her own a few times lately and I should probably make up for it."

Daniel and I say goodbye to Mum and Dad, and we both head out the door. He jumps in his car, and I start walking to the road.

Levi is in his driveway. "Katie, want a lift?"

What is it with everyone wanting to give me lifts?

"I'm fine. But thanks," I call over my shoulder.

I keep walking quickly with my head down, feeling a bit naked without my glasses on.

Something

Jessica is at the bus stop before me, and she smiles as I approach. "No glasses?"

"I'm giving the contacts another go," I say.

"Cool. You look really pretty today. Your hair is nice."

"Karen made me," I say, and we both laugh.

"You okay after Friday?" Jessica raises her eyebrows.

I sigh. "Yeah. It was … intense. But I'm alive."

"You survived Veronica."

"Yeah." I laugh again, but I'm not sure it's all that funny.

"How'd you and Karen go dress shopping?" Jessica asks as the bus pulls up. We climb on and take our usual seats.

"I found the perfect dress." I dump my bag on the floor and pull out my phone. "Look."

Jessica takes the phone and stares at the photo. "Oh my God. It's totally you."

"I know." My stomach fills with happy feelings.

"And so not what any of those snobs would wear."

"I know!" I can't contain my excitement and I squeal.

"Mum's taking Josie and me shopping this Thursday." Jessica scrunches her nose up. "I'd rather poke hot sticks in my eyes."

"Want me to come?"

"Nah. Mum wants to do the mother–daughter thing. Stacey is so disappointed."

We plug our headphones in and listen to music on the way to the station, where we meet up with Karen. I'm glad to be catching the train, because it means I have a little more time before any potential fallout from the weekend.

School is buzzing with activity when we arrive, and

after we swipe in, Jessica and I say goodbye to Karen and head towards art class. Marking for our major works is next week, and I have a few final touches I want to put on mine.

Veronica is in our class, and she glares at me when she walks in. I do my best to ignore her, but I'm on edge, waiting for her to use her whip-like tongue. Mrs Moran's presence seems to be enough to keep Veronica at bay though, and the room is quiet as everyone works on their art.

When planning my work, I decided to combine my love for reading with something I don't particularly like— fashion. Mrs Moran wanted us to challenge ourselves, so I designed a dress made entirely from old books. I'm really happy with how the gown has turned out, and I'll find out after marking if my work will make it into the Art Express exhibition at the National Art Gallery.

"She's itching to say something to you," Jessica whispers.

I glance up and she nods towards Veronica.

"Yeah, I bet she is." I turn back to my work. "But what's she going to say that she hasn't already?"

I push Veronica and the weekend from my mind and spend the first two periods checking all my paper folds, making sure the glue has set properly in the most important places. Then I add a paper rose, coated in broken gold-leaf, to the waist. I want to do well because even though Mum and Dad are expecting me to get a degree in law or medicine, what I really want to do is fine art. I haven't told them I want to apply for the Sydney College of Fine Arts. I'll cross that bridge when I come to it.

The bell goes, and I'm starting to think this project

will never feel finished. But I have another art class later this week, so I can fix anything then if I need to.

Math class is more revision and discussion, and when recess starts I'm glad to get back outside. It's short-lived though, and we're inside again for English then History. I haven't seen Veronica since Art, and when I walk into History I cringe.

She's sitting in her usual seat with Levi beside her. I pay no attention to either of them and drop into my chair next to Karen. Until now, no one besides Karen and Jessica has commented on my hair, or the fact I'm not wearing glasses.

"Look who's had a makeover," Veronica says.

A few snickers move around the room, but I stay facing forward and ignore them.

"I wonder how she could afford to do that," Rachel says.

"She probably begged for handouts." Veronica laughs.

I close my eyes and take a deep breath. She's almost right, except for the begging part.

"Ignore them," Karen whispers. "You look hot."

I open my eyes and smile at her, then I look over my shoulder and my gaze connects with Levi's. He's slouched in his chair, a pen in one hand, and his elbow on the desk.

"I like it," he says. "Looks nice." He smiles, and I can't help smiling back.

Mr Jenkins walks in and I turn to the front again, Levi's compliment warming my insides. I look down at the book on my desk, my smile falling away. *Concentrate, Katie.* I can't afford distractions now. Final exams are getting closer. I'll know in a couple of weeks if I made dux, but I still have to get the best mark I can in my final exams to get into university. *Stop getting distracted by boys. Or one particular boy.*

The rest of class feels like it goes on for an eternity, but at least I don't get any more comments from Veronica. Mr Jenkins talks too much for that to happen.

When the lunch bell rings, Karen and I are out of there as quickly as we can. We meet up with Jessica and Stacey, and I flop onto the grass, wishing the day would end so I could go home.

"I heard you had a rough weekend." Stacey bites into her sandwich.

"It wasn't so bad," I say. "It could've been worse."

Karen snorts. "Levi was a royal arse."

I don't disagree with her. "We found formal dresses though."

"Yes, we did." Karen smiles. "And Katie is going to knock everyone right out of their fancy high heels."

I blush and stare at the sandwich in my hand. "The only thing missing is a date."

"None of us have dates. You can be mine," Karen says.

Jessica clears her throat. "Um ... I might have someone."

Karen's eyes go wide. "What?"

"Who?" I ask.

"When did this happen?" Stacey stares at Jessica with wide eyes.

She shrugs. "Matthew O'Conner may have asked me."

"I can't believe you didn't tell me this morning." I smack her on the arm.

"Not bad." Karen smiles. "He's an okay guy."

Jessica blushes, and we tease her some more. Matthew

really is nice. I see him around school all the time, but we've never had a conversation. He keeps to himself a lot, even though he's in the rich league. I guess it just doesn't go to some people's heads.

"I think you should go with Levi." Karen looks at me.

"What the hell for?" I say, even though I want to. "He's been nothing but *wonderful* to me for the past few years. Why would I want to go with him?"

"Because you're in love with him," Stacey says.

I tear chunks of grass from the ground and throw them at her. "I'm not in love with him."

Jessica snorts. "Are you serious? You've been in love with him since kindergarten."

I take a deep breath because she's right, only I don't want to admit it to my friends. I'm not sure why I don't want to—I just don't. Maybe if I admit to being in love with Levi, it will make the whole situation seem worse. Can I trust him? I don't know if he's just a charmer, or if he's being genuine.

"Hey, Katie?" Veronica's voice travels across the oval, hitting my eardrums like a pick to ice.

I turn in her direction. "What?"

"Come and join us."

Veronica and her group are sitting where they usually do, on the edge of the oval in the best part of the yard. It's the best, because it's the hardest place for the on-duty teacher to see while doing rounds. And because it gets a nice mix of sun and shade.

I have no intention of getting up. "No thanks." I turn back to my small and safe group of friends.

"Oh no, here she comes," Stacey says.

When I reluctantly look over my shoulder again, Veronica is striding towards us, her nose in the air and her bitch-face on.

"You're acting like I was giving you a choice," she says when she reaches us.

I get to my feet and face her. Right now, she's my least favourite person. Ever. And I want to give it to her so badly, but I also don't want to stoop to her level. Despite the other day at the shops, I think I usually do a pretty good job of being nice, so I'm not going to let her change me into someone I'm not.

I take another deep breath. "Why do you want me to join you?"

"We're playing again. Thought you'd be up for the challenge."

"I'm a bit tired of your games, Veronica. Think I'll pass."

She stares at me and I can have a pretty good guess at what she's thinking. Someone like me shouldn't talk like this to someone like her. God forbid I should say no, or even think about standing up for myself.

"Well, it's back to me again, and I choose you," Veronica says.

Karen gets to her feet, and I'm surprised she even waited this long. She squares her shoulders, and Veronica raises her chin.

"If the words truth or dare come out of your mouth, I swear to God I will punch you in the face." Karen steps towards the queen bitch.

Veronica smirks, then she opens her mouth.

Oh God, Karen is going to hit her.

"Veronica," Levi says.

Something

I look over her shoulder at him. He's sitting on the grass with his legs stretched out in front of him, leaning back on his hands.

When Veronica doesn't answer, he calls her name again.

"Your leader is calling you," Karen says.

"He's not my leader." Veronica scowls.

"Ronnie, don't waste your breath," Jarred calls.

She still doesn't move.

"I'm not playing," I say. "You can do whatever you want to me, but you know what? I don't care. Because nothing you do to me rates on my importance scale. You can embarrass me, call me a bitch, whatever—but I'll still be better than you, because I don't use my money to buy my friends."

"That's because you haven't got any." Veronica puts her hands on her hips. "Money, or friends." She turns and stalks back towards her group.

"You do so have friends," Jessica says in her small voice.

"She's a total air waster," Karen says. "Ignore her."

We sit back down, but this time I angle myself so I don't have my back to Veronica and her group. I want to be able to see what's going on. I may have told her I don't care, but that's a big call. She could still jeopardise my chance at dux. *Please, leave me alone.*

"He's looking at you," Karen says.

She's sitting across from me, pulling bits of grass from the ground and rolling them between her fingers.

"He is not." I sneak a look at Levi from under my lashes.

"He totally is," Stacey says.

"Yeah." Jessica smiles at me. "We've both known Levi

a long time, and I reckon he's got the hots for you."

"Levi and me ... not going to happen," I say.

Karen sits up straighter. "What is going on now?"

A shadow falls over my legs, and I look up to see Geoff staring down at me.

I freeze.

"Knick off," Karen says. "You're blocking our sun."

He doesn't listen. Instead, he sits on the grass beside me.

"How are you, Katie?" he asks.

Someone who hasn't said a nice word to me ever has just asked how I am. What am I supposed to say?

"I'm fine." I draw my legs up and cross them.

"What do you want?" Karen asks.

"Gee, defensive much?" Geoff says.

"Do you blame us?" Stacey asks. "Your group doesn't exactly talk to ours, unless you're daring us to do something stupid."

"He mustn't be feeling well," Jessica says.

"I'm amazed at how different you and Josie are." Geoff stretches his legs out in front of him and leans back on his hands.

"Yeah, Jess is nice. Josie ... isn't," Karen says.

Geoff raises his eyebrows. "I've come to ask a question, actually."

The four of us stare at him, waiting for him to say whatever it is he came over to say. He smirks.

"Is this some kind of dare?" Stacey asks.

Karen glares at Geoff. "The answer is no."

"I haven't even asked the question yet," he says.

"You don't have to."

Something

I brace myself. I want to sink into the ground and disappear. Almost everyone around us is watching. I don't like being the centre of attention.

I go to open my mouth when Levi grabs Geoff by the collar.

"Get up." Levi pulls Geoff to his feet.

Geoff scowls and Levi shoves him away from us. They move out of earshot and have an animated discussion. Jarred joins them. Levi clenches his fists a few times, and I think maybe he wants to hit Geoff.

"What is that all about?" Karen asks.

I pick at the grass. "I don't want to know."

"Sure you do," Stacey says. "Levi looks angry."

"He's not the only one," I say.

"You okay?" Karen asks.

"First Veronica, now Geoff. Why can't they just leave me alone? Surely they have something better to do. Why do you guys even hang out with me, anyway?" I ask, looking around at my friends. "All of you could be one of the popular girls if you didn't pity me so much."

"We do not pity you!" Karen throws a handful of grass at me.

"She's right," Stacey says. "We don't. We know how awesome you are."

"You don't compare to them," Jessica says. "Don't even try to justify why they're bitches. They just are."

"And here we go again," Karen says.

Levi walks over to us, his hands stuffed in his pockets. Geoff and Jarred go back to their group at the end of the oval. Geoff glances over his shoulder a few times on his way.

"Either move or go away." Karen flicks her hand at Levi. "Preferably go away."

When I look up, my gaze meets Levi's and he smiles. I love and hate that smile all at the same time. I love it because it reminds me of how we used to be such good friends, but I hate it because now, after everything that's happened, I don't trust it. I can't tell if his smile is the old him or the new one.

"Katie?" he says.

"Yes?"

He runs a hand through his hair and my heart flutters. "Want to go for a walk?"

"With you?"

He looks around and chuckles. "Um ... yeah. With me."

"Is this another dare?" I ask.

He frowns. "Really? That's what you think?"

"Do you blame her?" Karen gets to her feet.

"No, it's fine." I get up, too. "Let's walk."

Levi moves towards the middle of the oval. I fold my arms over my chest and follow. When Levi reaches the cricket pitch, he stops. He's taken me right out in the open where everyone can see the two of us standing together. I imagine every set of eyes in the entire school staring at me and laughing. If I thought everyone looking when Geoff was sitting with us was bad, this is a million times worse.

"What's this all about?" I ask.

"You look really pretty today." Levi stares at his feet.

I scoff. "Seriously? And how can you tell? You're not even looking at me."

Levi raises his head. His brow creases but a small

smile plays at his lips. "I mean it, Katie. Your hair is really nice. And I can see your eyes better without your glasses."

I lick my lips. "You brought me to the middle of the oval to compliment me on my hair and eyes?"

Levi takes one hand from his pocket and rubs his forehead. I want him to run it through his hair, and then I want to run my fingers through his hair, but I clutch my sides with my hands and frown at him instead.

"I want to ask you something," he says.

"Funny, Geoff said the same thing."

"Geoff was being an arse."

"And you're being …?" I roll one hand through the air.

"Can I take you out this weekend? Saturday night?"

For a moment, it feels like everyone around us heard Levi's question and they stop talking. There's a vacuum of silence in my ears before the roar of noise rushes back in a second later.

"You want to take me out?" I ask.

"Yes."

"On a date?"

Levi smiles. "We can call it that if you like."

I bite my lip. He seems to want to make up for how he's treated me, so maybe I should let him. "Okay."

"Okay?"

"Yeah," I say. "If you promise not to be a jerk."

Levi chuckles. "I promise."

My stomach flip-flops. I feel like I'm getting in way over my head, but my heart—it's hoping for the fairy-tale ending I've always wanted.

What will I be getting myself into?

Getting through the rest of the week was torture. Four days felt like four months, and now that it's Saturday night, I'm a nervous wreck.

I'm nervous, because Levi is taking me out on a date. Which Daniel has been reminding me of for the past two hours.

"The day has finally come." My brother stands in my doorway, a grin on his face.

"What day is that?" I fling my Converse back into my wardrobe.

"The day my little nerdy sister is going on a date."

"It's not a date."

Daniel laughs. "You really have no clue."

"I have enough of a clue. I'm just in denial."

I dig around the bottom of my wardrobe for my strappy

brown sandals. Levi told me to wear something nice, but as to the level of niceness, I'm not sure how nice I should go. I have no idea where he's taking me, or what he has planned, so I've dressed in my usual jeans, with the new paisley top I bought with Karen. I find the sandals and sit on my bed to put them on.

"Have fun." Daniel goes to his room.

The doorbell rings a few minutes later. I glance at the clock above my desk. The hour hand ticks over to seven pm. He's right on time.

I fish my favourite amethyst ring from the little dish on my desk, slipping it onto my finger, then grab my phone and purse, and race down the stairs to find Mum already answering the door.

Levi steps over the threshold. "You look really nice, Katie."

"Thanks." Heat prickles my cheeks.

"Remember your curfew," Dad says from the lounge room.

"Yes," I mumble. "Bye, Mum." I give her a kiss on the cheek.

Levi and I walk across to his place and down the driveway to where his BMW is parked on the street.

"That's a pretty top," he says. "It brings out the green bits in your eyes."

My cheeks grow hotter, and my hands go clammy. Why am I so nervous? It's Levi. The guy I've known my whole life. The guy who used to be my best friend. The guy who shut me out because I have no money. The guy who is now the captain of the most prestigious high school in the shire.

Yep, that's why I'm nervous.

I stop at the car and frown.

Levi opens the door, but I don't get in.

"What's the matter, Katie?"

"I ..." I bite my lip. "Are you sure you want to take me out?"

"I wouldn't have asked you if I didn't want to." Levi smiles. "But we can stay home if you like?"

I shake my head. When I get in the car, the most amazing spicy smell hits my nose. It's coming from the back seat, and I turn to see what it is.

Levi climbs in behind the wheel. "Dinner. You like Thai, don't you?"

I nod and settle into the leather seat. Levi starts the car and we drive towards the highway.

"Where are you taking me?" I ask.

"You'll see." And he doesn't offer any more information than that.

We drive for ten minutes then Levi makes a right-hand turn into a side street. He pulls over and parks at the kerb. There's a park on the corner. I remember coming here when we were kids, but I haven't been for years. We drive past it every time we go to the shops, but it always goes unnoticed. I'm curious what Levi is up to.

"You have to promise me you won't look," Levi says.

"Are we having a picnic?"

"Just ... don't look, okay?"

"Sure. I won't."

"Great. Wait here."

Levi gets out and opens the back door, grabbing the food from the seat. He also opens the boot, and I pull my phone out to distract myself so I'm not tempted to watch him. After about ten minutes I wonder when he's going to come and get me. I glance up and he's walking towards my side of the car. Levi opens my door and looks down at me.

"You have to close your eyes for this part," he says.

I clutch my phone and my purse, and get out of the car. My legs are a little shaky because not only am I nervous, but I'm scared, too. I keep having visions of Veronica jumping from behind the bushes and yelling 'truth or dare'. Then I giggle, because, really?

"What's the joke?" Levi asks.

I smile. "Nothing. Closing my eyes now." I hug my purse and phone to my chest.

Levi takes my elbow and I move a few steps, hear the car door close, then take a couple more steps.

"Foot up," Levi says, pressing one hand into the small of my back and holding my arm with the other. "That's it. Hang on. I have to open a gate."

Metal squeals.

I shuffle my feet. "Are we almost there?"

"Just another couple of steps." Levi stops and gently turns my shoulders. "Okay, open your eyes."

At first, I'm not sure what I'm looking at. I blink a few times, and draw in a deep breath. We're standing in the middle of the park under a huge gum tree. The playground is to our left and the grassed area is on our right. On the ground is a picnic rug surrounded by tea-light candles. They flicker orange. Levi has set out our Thai dinner with plates and cutlery, and there are pink flowers scattered across the rug and around the candles.

I take a few steps closer, amazed that he has done something like this for me.

"Bougainvillea flowers," I say.

The biggest grin splits his face. "Do you like it?"

How do I answer that? I bite my lip and grip my purse before wrapping my arms around my waist. Tears prick the backs of my eyes.

Levi comes up behind me and puts his hands on my shoulders, pressing his lips to the back of my head.

"I'm so sorry for ... everything," he says.

I shudder with the effort of holding back the tears. "No one has ever done anything like this for me before," I whisper. "Thank you."

"You can thank me by helping me eat all this food." Levi takes my hand, and we sit on the rug.

For an hour, I forget about everything. Veronica and her stupid games. Who and what has hurt me in the past. None of it matters right now. All that matters is Levi and me, enjoying each other's company with no one else around to ruin it.

I don't want to ask Levi why he decided to do this for me. I don't want to think about anything other than spending time with him, because maybe there is something between us. Maybe I just need to let it happen and see where it goes.

The food is delicious, and I feel like I've eaten enough for three people. I pick up some of the bougainvillea flowers and twirl them between my fingers. I smile, so happy in this moment, sitting in a kid's park with the boy I've loved since I was a kid.

"Remember I said I shut you out because you don't fit

with my friends?" Levi looks at me with intense eyes.

I frown. "Why do you want to talk about this now?" Anger sparks in my chest, because he's ruining the moment.

"Just, listen." Levi runs his hand through his hair in that way I love so much. "I was wrong. *They* don't fit with you. I realise now I made the wrong choice."

"Yeah, you did. You broke my heart." I drop the flowers and stare at my hands, picking at my fingernails. The moment is totally gone.

"I was an idiot, that's all. Too wrapped up in trying to be the perfect … whatever. Can you forgive me?"

I stare at the flowers on the rug in front of me. Tears well in my eyes again, and the pink outlines of the flowers blur until they're nothing but splotches.

"That depends." I look up and our eyes meet. "Can you forgive yourself?"

"You know what the hardest part was?" Levi stares at me for a few heartbeats, then looks away. "I went through a pretty rough time after Mason died. I'm still going through it. And I wanted to talk to you, but I didn't know how to fix things between us. I didn't know if you would ever speak to me again."

I adjust my position and draw my legs up to my chest, resting my chin on my knees. "I was worried about you. I wanted to talk to you at the funeral, but I figured you didn't want me to be there for you. I would've been though."

"There's no excuse for the way I've treated you."

I hug my knees tighter, and stare at Levi. "The past is the past. It is what it is. We can't change it."

Levi reaches out and takes my hand, giving it a gentle squeeze. "How can you be so forgiving? You must hate me."

"I don't *hate* anyone. What's the point in holding a grudge? It only makes you unhappy." I stare at our hands, Levi's fingers entwined in mine. "I hate what you did, but I don't hate you. I could never ..." I let my unfinished words hang between us, listening to the occasional car passing on the road beside the park.

"I don't deserve your forgiveness," Levi finally says. "You're really something, you know that, Katherine Sullivan?" Levi lets go of my hand and starts packing up the food. "We should go. We have a movie to see. Unless you want to stay here?"

"A movie sounds perfect." I smile.

Levi pulls me to my feet, and we pack everything back into the car. Part of me wants to be happy that he's trying so hard to fix things between us, but there's another part of me that can't help doubting his motivations. What if he breaks my heart again? Especially now he's holding so much of it?

I stood up to Veronica.

I'm brave—much braver than I'd ever thought I could be.

Maybe it's time I trust myself to trust Levi. I'm strong enough for this—and he's lucky to have me in his life. I decide to start trusting him and see where it gets me.

Levi parks on the middle level of the car park and we walk out past the restaurants then upstairs to the cinema.

"Action, romance, or drama?" Levi asks.

I look up at the titles rolling across the board above the ticket sales counter. I don't mind what we see. I just want to sit alone with Levi for a while and forget about the rest of the world.

Something

"You choose," I say. "And don't pick romance because it's what you think I want to watch."

"Action then?" Levi laughs.

He gets the biggest box of popcorn he can, and pays for our tickets, holding my hand as we walk to cinema five. We sit in the back row, and when the lights go down my heartrate quickens.

I'm nervous all over again.

Levi lifts the armrest between us and I stiffen.

"Relax," he whispers in my ear.

I settle into the crook of his arm and stare at the screen, but if someone were to ask me what the movie was about, I wouldn't be able to tell them. I'm too preoccupied with savouring the feeling of Levi's arm around me, and the way his body moves in response to the movie.

Disappointment settles into my stomach when the movie finishes, because it means it's time to go and I won't have Levi's arm around me anymore. Reluctantly, I move out of his embrace and we leave the cinema.

"We still have a couple of hours before your curfew," Levi says. "What do you want to do?"

I glance around the foyer of the cinema at all the people leaving. Most of them are couples like Levi and me. What troubles have they been through? I hope theirs haven't been as hard as ours. Seeing how happy they are makes me smile.

"Hot chocolate?" I say. "The café should still be open."

"Chocolate café it is then."

Levi puts his arm around my shoulders and pulls me close. We walk out into the mall.

He stops us at the clock fountain in the centre and pulls

a twenty-cent piece from his pocket, handing it to me.

"Make a wish," he whispers in my ear.

I'm not sure I believe in making wishes, so I think about what would make me happy instead. I feel the weight of the coin in my palm before I toss it in. It makes a little splash as it hits the water. When it sinks to the bottom and settles with the other coins, I stare at it for a moment. The coins glisten under the mall lighting like a star-filled sky.

I wish Levi and I will become something special.

We continue on to the café and I order my favourite. A white hot chocolate with two marshmallows on the side. Levi orders a dark hot chocolate, and we find a quiet table at the back of the café, away from the other patrons.

Levi takes a sip of his drink and smirks. "You have a froth moustache. It's cute."

I lick my lips and return his smile.

We spend an hour talking about our childhoods, and reminiscing about the stupid stuff we used to get up to.

We had such a good time together back then. Before high school, and Veronica, and Mason's death …

Mason.

Is he the reason Levi fights with his dad?

I don't know exactly what's going on, but something isn't right between them. I stare at the dark scab on the corner of Levi's lip. He's had drunken injuries before— maybe this is just another one.

I don't want to ruin the night by asking questions I probably shouldn't, so I focus on Levi's intense eyes and warm smile, as we remind each other of what we used to have.

Something

By the time we're ready to leave, we're both laughing. It feels good.

Our drive home is quiet. I don't want to talk too much because I don't want to say anything that will break the spell that seems to have fallen over us. The night has been pretty perfect, and I don't want to spoil it. I stare out the window and watch the lights pass as we make our way off the highway and towards home.

Levi parks in his driveway and walks me to my front door. It's fifteen minutes before curfew, and I'm not ready for the night to end. I face Levi and chew my lip, still not wanting to say anything that's going to ruin tonight.

We didn't watch a romance, but I've seen plenty of romantic movies, and this is the part when the goodnight kiss is supposed to happen. My heart beats faster, and my palms get sweaty. I hug myself and stare at my feet. I'm not sure I want to go there just yet. Kissing Levi is definitely on my to-do list, but now that he's standing in front of me, staring at me, all I want to do is run away and hide. The anticipation, the look in his eyes—they're making me nervous.

"I should go inside." I fumble my keys from my purse.

"Katie." Levi puts his hand over mine. "I won't kiss you if you don't want me to."

"Oh … you were going to …" I stare at our hands, heat rising into my cheeks.

I want to say something else, but no words come to mind. What am I supposed to say? Yes, kiss me? This is what I've been afraid of—ruining everything. And it looks like I'm going to do it by keeping my mouth shut this time.

"I don't want to ruin the night," I finally say.

Levi steps closer and puts a hand on my cheek, brushing my skin with his thumb. "That's not even possible."

He leans in, and my heart beats so fast I think I might go into cardiac arrest. Gently, he brushes my lips with his. He doesn't open his mouth, or use any force, and the feeling of his lips on mine sends tingles down my spine and all the way to my toes.

He pulls away, his thumb still caressing my cheek, and I stare at him with no words to describe the way he makes me feel. He moves his hand around to the back of my neck and twists his fingers into my hair, pressing his forehead to mine.

"Can I ask you something?" Levi says.

I close my eyes. "Sure."

"Will you ...?" He shuffles his feet. "Do you want to go to the formal with me?"

I pull away, and Levi untangles his hand from my hair. He raises his eyebrows and smiles.

I'm not sure what to say. "I ..."

The front door opens and Mum peers out at us. "Katie? I thought I heard voices."

"Sorry, Mum. I was just coming in."

"Don't be too long. Good night, Levi."

She leaves the door open, and I watch through the screen as she goes back upstairs.

"Thanks for a really nice night." I open the screen door and step inside. "I'll see you at school?"

Levi nods, his smile faltering. "Okay. See you Monday. Want a lift?"

"I'll go with Karen and Jess. Night."

I close the door before he walks away, unsure why I

didn't give him an answer to his question. He seems genuine, but maybe it's safer if I go to the formal without a date. I've pretty much already resigned myself to the fact that that's how it's going to be anyway.

I don't want to say no, but if I say yes, what will I be getting myself into?

12

Who I am

*F*or the next couple of weeks everyone is in full-on study and revision mode. Levi asks about the formal again, but I make it clear I can't think about anything other than exams. I want to say yes, but it all seems too good to be true. What if I agree to go with him and then everything comes crashing down around me?

I travel to school with Jessica and Karen, even though Levi offers to drive me every morning. It makes it easier to avoid giving him an answer, and I don't want to completely abandon my friends.

Today, when I get to school the halls are buzzing with talk of the formal, which is a little over a week away. Discussions about dresses, corsages, and cars are coming out of the mouths of every year twelve student I pass. I don't get why it's such a big deal, today of all days.

Something

Today is Year Twelve Awards day.

Today is the day we're on show to the entire school and our families.

Today is the day I find out if I made dux or not.

"Today is the day my life could potentially be over," I say to Karen as we make our way to the hall where the entire school is assembling for a big morning of presentations, awards, and performances.

"Stop worrying. You'll romp it in," Karen says. "No one here is smarter than you. Besides, there are more important things to discuss."

"Like what?" I stare at her blankly.

"Jess doesn't have shoes to go with her dress yet," she says. "Apparently, she couldn't find any when her mum took her and her witch sister shopping."

"You're talking about shoes at a time like this?" I glare at her.

"Calm down. I told you, you've got this." Karen grabs my hand and we make our way to the front of the hall to our assigned seats. The back section of the hall has seating set out for the parents and family members who are able to attend a ceremony during the day—which is a lot of them, since they're all so rich and can afford the time off work. Mum is here, but Dad had to go to a service call at a building in the city. Something about a burst water pipe that flooded the main electrical board.

Everyone is settled by ten am. We sit through the headmistress's boring speech and a host of awards for various things from sport to citizenship.

Then the academic awards begin. They start with individual subject awards, and Veronica receives an award for academic excellence in Biology. I don't take Biology, so I'm not too concerned. I lean forward. What award will be announced next? Will I get first in any subjects?

"Would you stop it?" Karen whispers. "Sit back."

I try to relax into my chair, but I'm eagerly awaiting the next announcement.

My name is called for academic excellence in Visual Arts, History, and Advanced English. My face hurts from smiling as I walk on stage to shake the headmistress's hand and take my certificates. I spot Mum clapping and smiling as I return to my seat.

There are a few more announcements, then Mrs Pritchard adjusts the microphone.

"Now, the moment everyone has been eagerly awaiting," she says. The hall falls silent. "The student I'm about to announce has been a pleasure to have amongst us for the past two years. She has gone above and beyond to ensure her academic achievements have been of the highest standard."

I tense in my chair. It has to be me. *Just spit it out.*

"This school prides itself on accepting only the best," she continues. "Each year we offer one place to an exceptional student who undergoes rigorous screening for our scholarship program, and this year that student has earned the award of dux. Please put your hands together for Katherine Sullivan."

The hall erupts into applause.

Karen slaps me on the arm. "Get up there."

I stand, and my legs wobble as I walk to the stage. Mrs Pritchard shakes my hand again and congratulates me, then leads me to the lectern.

I've tried not to think about this part too much.

I've been so caught up in everything that's been happening, with study, and Levi, and the formal, it seems like I wrote my speech years ago.

I put my certificate on the surface in front of me, then take the piece of paper from my pocket and unfold it. When I look out into the crowd I see a lot of faces I don't know, some I do, and some I don't like very much. Veronica is sitting with her arms folded, and a scowl on her face. Levi is at the head of the first row of year twelves, waiting to give his captain's speech after me.

Our gazes lock, and he smiles. I take a deep breath.

"Mrs Pritchard, teachers, fellow students, parents." I pause, and Levi gives me a nod. "I'm humbled and grateful to receive this award, but I want you all to know that getting here has not been easy. It took a lot of hard work, but most of all, it took determination. It's not easy being the one who is at a disadvantage, where every obstacle thrown your way is bigger than the last." A few students shift in their seats. "If this school and its students have taught me one thing, it's that no matter who we are, where we come from, or what our position in life is, there is nothing we can't do. We can and will achieve great things with determination, and the belief that no one but ourselves can stop us. Thank you."

More applause sounds around the hall, and Mum stands, clapping furiously. I step away from the lectern and a flash goes off, sending spots across my vision, but I can't help grinning. The photographer clicks away a couple more times before letting me leave the stage. By the time I return to my seat my cheeks ache from smiling so wide.

"Way to go," Karen says, nudging me. "You really gave it to them."

I guess I did. I'm not sure if I'll get any backlash for implying that I didn't have a fair playing field, but I'm not sure I even care. What's the worst they can do? Take the award away from me?

Mrs Pritchard calls Levi to the stage to give his captain's speech. After addressing the crowd, Levi locks his gaze on me, and he doesn't break it until he's finished. "Since our early days as year seven students, we've come so far, and achieved so much. We've laughed together, cried together, and grown together. I'm proud to be captain of such an outstanding group of young adults ready to take on the world. Because now, we are ready. And as Katie said, there is nothing we can't do. Congratulations to all our award receivers. Thank you."

Levi returns to his seat to another deafening round of applause. Mrs Pritchard declares the awards ceremony over, and we all file out of the hall to have lunch with our parents and friends.

Mum hugs me. "Congratulations, honey. You should have no trouble getting into university." She holds me at arm's length. "You'll make a great lawyer or doctor."

I smile and hug her again, but my stomach knots at the thought of telling her I don't really want to study law or medicine. Now is not the time to bring it up though.

Mum hangs around for a while, along with everyone else, and I'm grateful when people start to leave. It quietens down a bit and I can go and sit with my friends.

Something

I lie back on the grass and stare up at the clear spring sky.

"Has he asked you yet?" Karen says. She's sitting behind me, running her fingers through my hair.

I shade my eyes and stare at a solitary cloud drifting across the sky. It looks like a heart, if I tilt my head sideways.

"He has," I say.

"What? And you didn't tell me? When? What did you say?" Karen stops playing with my hair and stares down at me.

"She hasn't given me an answer yet." Levi stands over us, blocking the sun. "She's left me hanging."

I sigh and sit up, crossing my legs. Levi plonks his backpack on the grass and sits beside me.

"You should answer him," Stacey says. "I want to know what you'll say."

"She's going to say yes," Karen says.

"I'm right here." I glare at her.

"Me too." Levi smiles.

Jessica laughs. "Leave them alone."

"Why?" Karen asks. "They obviously need help with this."

Levi throws a twig at her and it lands in her hair. She screws her nose up as she picks it out and throws it back at him.

I dip my head and let my fringe fall around my face. I don't want to make a big deal out of this. No one has ever asked me to a dance before, I've always gone on my own, and I don't want the fuss. I also don't know if I should say yes to Levi. I've been avoiding answering him, because what if it's the wrong decision? I'm so scared that none of this is real.

Levi reaches over and tucks my hair behind my ear. My cheeks grow hot and I want to hide again.

He leans over and whispers in my ear, "Want to take a walk?"

I glance at him and nod. Levi jumps up and offers me his hand. I take it and he pulls me to my feet, putting one arm around my shoulders and tucking me in to his side. I don't look to see if anyone is watching us, but they probably are.

"Where are we going?" I ask.

"You'll see."

Levi leads me to the far side of the oval. Being over here isn't breaking the rules, but not many students bother to come this far away from the comfort of the shaded seats. There's nothing here anyway, and I wonder where he's taking me.

We reach the fence and Levi looks around before jumping over. "Come on." He motions for me to follow.

"Um ... we're not supposed to jump the fence, Levi."

"Don't make me throw you over it." He smiles. "Seriously, it's fine. I come here all the time. And the on-duty teacher just walked around the main building, so hurry up before she comes back."

I pivot and hoist myself onto the metal fence. "Turn around. I don't want to flash you."

Levi laughs, but he does as I ask. I put one leg over and then the other, dropping the short distance to the ground on the other side. Levi takes my hand and we follow the fence for a few metres before taking a worn path that leads into the trees behind the admin block. The tall gums enclose a small clearing with a shaded patch of grass. Levi goes to one of the trees which has a hole in the trunk, the perfect size for a possum to live in, and pulls out a rolled up picnic rug.

"You brought me to the make-out room?" I ask.

"It's not what you think." Levi flicks the rug and lays it on the grass.

"Then tell me, what should I think?" I cross my arms and glare at him.

Levi sits and pats the rug next to him.

I don't move.

"Katie, I'm not—"

"I'm not making out with you."

"Why not? Making out is fun." He grins.

"I'm serious. Not here."

He grabs my hand and gently pulls until I'm kneeling and facing him. He runs circles over the back of my hand with his thumb, and I stare at our hands. His touch is so gentle.

"I just want to be with you," he says. "Without everyone staring at us. We don't have to do anything but sit."

I move so I'm sitting with my legs tucked beside me. Levi leans in and presses his forehead to mine. My breath catches in my throat. He closes his eyes, and I stare at the tip of his nose and his eyelashes. His face is so close to mine. His lips part, and his breath tickles my mouth.

I want him. But wanting him scares me.

I touch his lips with my thumb and press my palm to his cheek. "I'm scared," I whisper.

"Of what?" Levi asks. "You don't need to be scared."

"I don't know if I can control myself when I'm with you."

"I have the same problem." He keeps his eyes closed, but circles his arm around my waist and pulls my body closer to his.

"If I let myself … if I get too attached to you … I don't really have you yet, and I'm already scared of losing you."

Levi opens his eyes and pulls away to look at me. "You've always had me, Katie."

He uncrosses his legs and pulls me into his lap, hugging me with both arms. I've never been hugged like this by him, and it makes me feel safe. I lay my head on his shoulder and a hand on his chest, feeling the beat of his heart.

We sit like this until the next bell rings. We don't talk, or do anything, we just sit. And it's comforting.

"We should go," I say.

We untangle ourselves and get to our feet. Levi rolls up the blanket and puts it back in the tree. Then he takes my hand and pulls me close for another hug. When he releases me, he has a smile on his face, and he raises his eyebrows.

"I'm only going to ask this once more. Katherine Sullivan, will you go to the formal with me?"

I mirror his smile. "Since you said you won't ask again, I guess I have to say yes."

"You could say no." He kisses the tip of my nose.

"But I thought you wanted a yes."

"What do you want?" he asks.

"I want … you."

Levi studies me. His mouth curls up on one side and he chuckles. "Thank you."

Something

"What for?" I ask.

Levi leads me back along the path to the oval. "Being you."

My smile grows, and my belly fills with little flutters.

For the first time in a while, I'm happy to be who I am.

So heartbreaking

*L*evi hardly leaves my side for the rest of the week, and Veronica backs off enough for me to think that maybe he has said something to her. I knuckle down and do as much study as I can, helping Levi as well, and before I know it the day of the formal is here.

Karen sets the hair curler on my desk and spins me to face her. She digs through the huge cosmetics bag she brought with her and pulls out a compact and a brush.

"Hair is gorgeous. Now for the makeup." She smiles.

"Not too much," I say. "I want to look like me."

"I promise, you'll look amazing."

She sets to work. I sit patiently in my desk chair while Karen brushes and smudges, and makes me pucker and blot my lips. No doubt Veronica and the other girls will be going to professional hairdressers and makeup artists to get ready. I'm so lucky I have Karen, and her makeup expertise.

After about half an hour, she says, "All done. Have a look."

I stare at myself in the full-length mirror on my wardrobe door. I'm not sure who the girl is looking back at me. It's me, but it isn't. I don't wear makeup, and it feels weird, but I like what Karen has done. It's not too heavy or too dark. There's just a hint of colour on my lips, and some rosiness in my cheeks. I smile at my reflection, twisting a finger into one of the curls Karen has set with the curler. They fall loosely around my shoulders.

"Thank you," I say. "It's perfect."

Karen smiles and busies herself working on her own makeup. I'm not much help in that department, so I lay out our dresses on the bed. When she's done, Karen helps me slip into my dress, and I help her with hers. She puts on a silver choker with a topaz teardrop that hangs from the centre. I don't have much jewellery, and I don't like too much bling, so Karen helps me fasten a silver chain around my neck. The pendant is a small heart with three diamonds in it, a gift from my parents a couple of years ago. Then I slip my favourite silver amethyst ring onto my right hand.

There's a light knock at the door, and Mum pokes her head in.

"Oh, Katie. You look wonderful," she says, tears glistening in her eyes. She comes into the room and hugs me. "You, too, Karen. Your gown is beautiful. You're both so grown-up."

"I guess you scrub up okay," Daniel says from the doorway.

"Gee, thanks." I poke my tongue out at him.

"What's going on in here?" Dad asks. "Well. It seems you have a dance to get to." He smiles and his eyes crinkle. "There's someone at the door waiting for you, Katie."

Karen and I make our way down the stairs with everyone else in tow. Karen's parents come out of the lounge room and look up the stairs at us, huge smiles on their faces.

Levi is standing at the front door, dressed in a traditional black cocktail suit. His tie is a deep purple, which complements my dress perfectly. I look at Karen, and she smiles.

"Someone had to coordinate you. I knew you'd forget," she says.

I stop at the bottom of the stairs and Levi takes the few steps to my side. He kisses me on the cheek and whispers in my ear, "You look beautiful."

"Thanks," I manage to say before Mum announces she wants photos.

"A couple on the stairs first," she says, shuffling Levi and I into position.

Mum snaps away, then she swaps Levi with Karen, and the two of us beam at the camera. I wish Jessica and Stacey could be here, too, but they're leaving from Jessica and Josephine's house. Hopefully our two cars will time it well enough to arrive at the formal at the same time.

Mum herds us out to the front yard for more photos. Levi tugs me gently towards the bougainvillea. The side of the house is a mass of pink blooms, and Levi wanting to have our photo taken in front of it makes my heart flutter with happiness. Dad frowns, but I beam back at him. I'm not going to let anything ruin this moment.

I feel bad for Karen though. She doesn't have a date, but if she's upset about it she's not showing it. She fixes a wide smile to her face, and it doesn't budge as we go next door to Levi's place.

"Hi, Yvonne," Mum says to Levi's mum as we enter the foyer. "Will Mark be joining the fun?"

"I'm afraid he has to work late," she says. "But I promised him photos, so come on, kids."

"Hold on, Mum." Levi grabs a small clear box off the hallstand and hands it to me. "This is for you."

Inside is a small wrist corsage. It's so simple, and it's beautiful—a cluster of three bougainvillea flowers surrounded by greenery and attached to a purple band.

I don't know what to say. Thank you doesn't seem enough, because he hasn't bought just any corsage—he's actually thought about it. I slip it onto my wrist and stand on my tiptoes to give Levi a kiss on the cheek. I don't care that our parents are watching.

Yvonne leads us through to the open-plan family room. Veronica and Jarred are waiting on the lounge, along with Geoff who is going solo. Veronica gives me a smug smile, and I'm not exactly sure how to read it. She stares down her nose, scrutinising me from head to toe before standing up.

Veronica's dress is nothing short of amazing. The cerise cocktail dress stops above her knees, showing off her long legs. The skirt is a mass of ruffles. Silver diamantes and beading cover the bodice, making her look as if she's dripping in diamonds. The spaghetti straps are also a row of sparkling gems. And I hate to admit it, but her silver stilettoes are perfect for the dress.

"You look really nice." I smile. No need to be a bitch when it's true.

"Thanks," she says. "Your dress is ... different. It's pretty."

"Thank you," I say, unsure if she's just being polite.

Levi's mum pulls the camera out again, getting us all to pose in front of the big windows, on the couch, and in every other place she can think of. Geoff and Karen end up standing together and looking like a couple, much to Karen's disgust.

"Everyone, please have a drink." Yvonne gestures to the kitchen counter where a line of champagne flutes sit, filled to the top with bubbly orange juice. Each glass has a strawberry on the rim. "There's more orange juice than champagne, so don't worry." She smiles.

Levi grabs two glasses, bringing one over to me. I sip my drink and watch everyone sipping theirs, nibbling at the finger food, dip, and crackers.

Mum comes over to me. "No more after this."

"Mum, relax," Daniel says. "It's Katie."

"What's that supposed to mean?" I ask.

Daniel shrugs and goes to get a glass and eat the food. Veronica sniggers.

The adults move into the lounge room and the rest of us hover around the food.

"We should toast," Karen says.

"To getting drunk." Geoff raises his glass.

Levi laughs.

"You're an idiot," Karen says.

Something

"To a good night." Levi takes a sip of his champagne.

"Don't drink yet." Karen grabs his arm. "To the future … and to not knowing where any of us will end up."

"Sounds good enough." Jarred raises his glass.

We all chink them together. Veronica even chinks me, but she smirks. I get the feeling she knows something I don't, and my stomach fills with dread. I realise that I'm nervous, only I don't have butterflies—I have bogon moths.

I smile at Levi and take a sip of my drink. The bubbles tickle my nose and I giggle. Levi downs his glass in one mouthful, and I catch his mum frowning from the other side of the room.

"You should pace yourself," Daniel says, sipping his drink. "Don't want to be drunk before you get there."

"I'm good." Levi eats the strawberry, then grabs the bottle from the bench and fills his glass. No orange juice this time.

"Champagne has a habit of going to your head."

"Don't be such a party pooper, Daniel," Veronica says.

Levi drinks this glass more slowly, but it still worries me.

Mum and Dad glance over a few times, and I smile at them, trying not to let on how uncomfortable I am around these people. It would be nice to go outside again.

Levi puts his lips to my ear. "I've got a bottle for the car. We can have more later."

The drunkest I've ever been was at Veronica's party, and I don't plan to get drunk again any time soon, especially after seeing how Levi is when he's had too many.

"The car is here," Yvonne says from the front window of the family room.

Levi grabs a bottle of champagne from the fridge, downs the rest of his drink, and sets the glass on the bench. The others do the same and start towards the foyer. I still have half a glass, and I don't like the idea of drinking it all at once, even if it is mostly orange juice.

Veronica glances over her shoulder and laughs.

I take one more sip of the bubbly drink, then set the glass on the bench before following the others.

Daniel grabs my elbow, and we stop in the foyer as everyone else goes outside. "You okay?"

"I wish you'd stop asking me that. I'm fine."

"Just ... be careful tonight. Please. Don't drink too much."

"Daniel—"

"Katie, you're my little sister. I worry about you."

"Well, don't." I grab his hand and pull him out the door towards the others.

"I could talk to him. You know ... warn him if he hurts you ..."

I stop on the path and glare at my brother. "Don't you dare."

He bursts out laughing, and that's when I realise he's joking. I smack him on the arm and join the group standing next to the black stretch Hummer.

Jarred opens the door and helps Veronica in. Geoff does the same for Karen, and I have to hide my look of shock. I've never seen him act so ... gentlemanly. Is it because he wants to be nice, or because the adults are watching us?

"After you." Levi rests his hand on the top of the door.

I kiss Mum and Dad.

Something

"Have fun sweetie," Mum says.

"No more drinking," Dad says.

Levi smiles. "I'll look after her."

I climb into the limo next to Karen. She's sitting across from Geoff, which means I'm directly facing Veronica. The fifty-minute trip to Sydney is going to be great. I quickly type a message to Jessica to tell them we're leaving.

The Hummer pulls out of the driveway and into the street, and Levi pops the bottle of champagne before we even reach the highway. He pours everyone a glass, then sets the empty bottle upside down in the cooler.

"Cheers," he says.

"To a great night," Geoff says.

Jarred smirks. "To truth."

I bite my lip, wondering what he means by that.

Levi takes my hand and gives it a squeeze, but I don't miss the glare he gives Jarred. Something is going on, and I have no idea what. *Why are they giving each other funny looks?*

The bogon moths return.

"To getting drunk." Veronica takes a big mouthful of champagne.

Karen snorts. "To getting out of the hellhole that is our school."

"To new beginnings," I say, clinking my glass against Levi's and taking a sip. "Maybe all of us could do with one of those."

He squeezes my hand again, and we settle back for the ride into the city. The conversation is light, and I listen or join in when I'm not staring out the window. Before I know it, we're crossing the bridge over the harbour.

I crane my neck to look up at the huge steel structure as we pass under it, and the prettiness of the lights makes me smile. The limo takes us through the tight and busy city streets, stopping at the base of Sydney Tower.

The boys get out and help the three of us from the car. Several limos arrive carrying other students from school, and all the girls look amazing. There's so much bling. I fiddle with my necklace as I glance around at the array of dresses.

We make our way into the foyer of the building, and the volume rises with the chatter of excited formal-goers. I don't want to talk to any of them. I'm overwhelmed, and I glance over my shoulder at the entry doors, looking for an exit.

Jessica and Stacey walk through as I'm planning my escape, and I take a deep breath. Now they're here, I have my three girls. Maybe I can get through this in one piece.

Jessica looks incredible in a floor-length royal blue gown. Exquisite pearl beading covers her décolletage and waist. Stacey wears a pale pink mermaid dress with a sheer back and sleeves. Delicate beading covers her shoulders and arms.

All my friends are stunning, and seeing them brings a tear to my eye.

The crowd begins to move, and we pile into the lifts to make the journey to the top of the tower. The theme for the formal is regal, and the thought actually makes me laugh. It's pretty fitting, because every rich kid here thinks they're royalty. The restaurant is decorated with rich purple, red, and gold. The tablecloths alternate in purple and red, with gold sequins and coloured gemstones scattered down the middle. Golden bows adorn the white chair covers. There's even a stage with two thrones for the crowning of the formal king and queen.

Many of the girls fit the royal theme with their full-length gowns. My dress doesn't look like something a queen would wear, with its long and short hemline, but I still feel like a princess, and I'm determined to have a good night.

As we walk through, we're directed to line up for photos before finding our seats. Levi takes my hand and we step in front of the deep purple velvet wall. A curtain of sparkling gold sequins hangs in front of it, giving it a magical touch.

"That's it," the photographer says. "Give her a hug."

Levi pulls me close and presses a kiss to my temple while the photographer snaps away. I stare up at him and smile, lost in his eyes.

"Okay, next," the photographer calls.

"Let's find our seats." Levi tugs my hand and leads me through the rows of tables.

We find our places near the dance floor and to the right of the stage. I'm pleased to see we're sitting with Karen, Jessica and her date, Matthew, and Stacey, but we also have Veronica, Jarred, Josephine, and Geoff. I guess it won't be too bad. I've survived Veronica and her friends for this long—another night isn't going to make a difference.

I scan the room and absorb it all. The people filing in. The teachers bustling about.

"We should do the photo booth later," I say to Levi, pointing to the back corner of the large room.

"Sure." Levi pulls his chair out and sits. "That'll be fun."

We chat amongst our table while we wait for everyone to be seated. Mrs Pritchard addresses us, not saying anything that hasn't already been said at awards day or graduation, and we groan at the parts we're supposed to and laugh at the other ones.

Once dinner is over the music starts pumping, and half the year hit the dance floor. I'm not much of a dancer, so I'm not that eager to get out there. Karen, Stacey, and I sit at the table for a while and watch the commotion around us. Levi is off talking to his mates on the far side of the room, and I'm actually in a good place, happy to sit back and watch life go by for a while, and not have to actively take part in it.

"How was your limo ride?" Stacey asks over the music.

"Not too bad," I say. "Veronica contained herself, if that's what you mean."

We all chuckle, then I slap Karen's arm and point towards the dance floor. Jessica is dancing with her date, Matthew, and her face is plastered with a huge smile. He tries to get close to her every chance he can, and seeing Jessica so happy makes me happy, too.

The music throbs through the floor and vibrates into my feet. It settles in the pit of my stomach, and the feeling isn't something I've experienced before. I'm happy at a school function. No one is being mean to me. Everyone is having a good time. I'm just another person in the crowd, and it feels great.

I jump up and grab Karen's hand, pulling her until

Something

she's on her feet. Stacey follows, and we go to the floor-to-ceiling windows and look out over the city. The lights streak through the darkness, creating a rainbow of movement. We're up so high in the tower, as if we're on top of the world. It's magical, and surreal, and amazing.

The music changes, and I feel someone's presence behind me.

"Would you like to dance?" Levi asks. He tucks his chin into my neck from behind.

I turn into his embrace. "With you? Yes."

Levi slips his hand into mine and leads me to the dance floor. He walks backwards, never taking his eyes off me. His gaze makes me feel as if I'm the only person he sees in the room. We reach the dance floor, and he pulls me close, wrapping his arms around me. I link my fingers together behind his neck, feeling safe in his embrace. We sway to the slow beat of the music, and I rest my head on his shoulder. His scent is like a warm summer's day, and I relax into him, like I would while lazing on the grass in the sun.

"Katie," Levi whispers in my ear.

I raise my head and stare into his eyes. He leans down and presses his lips to mine. I tense and my heart races, thumping against my ribcage, but when he doesn't pull away, I relax. He gently parts my lips with his tongue, and I grip the hair at the base of his neck. He deepens our kiss and I twist my fingers into his hair like I've always wanted to do, gripping the strands as passion courses through me.

Levi breaks away, and I take a deep breath.

"Wow," I say.

"Yeah." He smiles and kisses the tip of my nose. The music speeds up, and Levi leans down to put his mouth to my ear. "I'll be back in a minute."

I nod and look around for Karen. She's at our table with Jessica. When our gazes meet, Karen jumps up and drags Jessica with her over to where I am on the dance floor. Stacey joins us, and we smile and laugh at each other, dancing in our small group. We're having so much fun it's not until my feet start aching that I think it's time to sit down.

I tap Karen's arm and point towards our table, then move off the dance floor. The music pumps around us. I fall into my seat, a bead of sweat trickling down my back. I take my shoes off and dig my toes into the carpet.

"This is so much fun," Karen shouts over the music.

I smile wide because I don't disagree with her.

Jessica and Stacey drop into seats beside us and take their shoes off, too.

I lean towards Karen and yell, "Did you see where Levi went?" I search for him around the restaurant.

She shakes her head. "I think a few of the guys are out in the foyer near the lifts."

I scan the room again, but I can't see him anywhere.

"Back in a minute." I slip my shoes on.

I make my way around the room, looking for Levi, edging along the wall towards the archway that leads to the foyer section in front of the lifts. When I reach the arch, the music isn't as loud, and I hear voices. I stop before going through. I probably shouldn't listen in on someone else's conversation, but it's Geoff's voice, and I'm curious.

Something

"Katie really has no clue?" Geoff asks.

What are they talking about? Maybe Levi has something romantic planned for me. I smile and bite my lip, my stomach filling with little flutters.

"No," Levi says. "And she's never going to find out."

"You know it's not over yet." Jarred sounds as if he's smiling.

"You haven't completed the dare," Geoff says.

My breath hitches. My hands shake, and I flex my fingers to stop the trembling from spreading to the rest of my body.

"Taking Katie to the formal was only half the deal," Jarred says.

"I know." Levi's voice has an angry edge to it.

A laugh bubbles into my throat, but I suppress it, and I want to kick myself for being so stupid. Of course it was too good to be true.

As if Levi would ever have asked me to the formal of his own accord.

Talking to me again. Being nice. Taking me on a romantic date.

It's all been part of their stupid game.

Truth or dare has never been so heartbreaking.

Katie's story continues in ...

Nothing

All the Things: part two

Author's note and acknowledgements

The first draft I ever wrote for this book was way back in 2014. It was my NaNo novel, and at around 55k it wasn't anywhere near finished. It hadn't really gone in the direction I'd hoped, and being my first contemporary, I was scared. As a result, those words sat dormant on my hard drive for two years, until I decided to re-visit Katie's story. I had always wanted to write this book in three parts, so here is the first part done. It took me much thought and soul-searching to get this book to where it is now. There is a lot of me in this book, and even though it was a struggle to write at times, I hope you enjoyed reading it as much as I did (mostly) writing it. Katie's story isn't finished though, and I would love you to stick around to find out what happens.

As always, I have some people to thank.

First up are two amazing authors who I am proud to be able to call my friends. They are awesome beta readers, and my partners in crime. Selina Fenech and Serene Conneeley, you have both pushed me to be and do my very best. You give me support, make me focus, and encourage me to take action. Thank you for all the things. (See what I did there?)

My family: thank you for loving me no matter how crazy I can be, and for supporting my need to have my own space in the house where I can work and write.

Thanks to the Story Queens girls—you are an amazing bunch of women. I love our meetings, writing retreats, and online support network. You have all helped me improve and grow as a writer.

To my editor, Lauren Clarke, thank you once again for all the shiny words. I love your face.

And finally, to my readers, thank you from the bottom of my heart for reading the first part of Katie's story.

About the author

𝒦. 𝒜. 𝐿𝑎𝑠𝑡 was born in Subiaco, Western Australia, and moved to Sydney when she was eight. Artistic and creative by nature, she studied Graphic Design and graduated with an Advanced Diploma. After marrying her high school sweetheart, she concentrated on her career before settling into family life. Blessed with a vivid imagination, K. A. Last began writing to let off creative steam, and fell in love with it. She is currently studying her Bachelor of Arts at Charles Sturt University, with a major in English, and minors in Children's Literature, Art History, and Visual Culture. She now resides in the countryside on the mid-north coast of NSW with her family and a menagerie of animals.

Connect with K. A. Last

Website www.kalastbooks.com.au
Facebook www.facebook.com/KALastBooks
Instagram www.instagram.com/kalastbooks
Pinterest www.pinterest.com/kalast
Goodreads www.goodreads.com/KALast
Twitter www.twitter.com/KALastBooks

**Scan the code to subscribe to
K. A. Last's newsletter.**

Available Now

Is love
really
worth
the fall?

THE TATE CHRONICLES

Scan for more
information

Available Now

**Do you have a story idea
but don't know how to start writing?**

A Novel Idea! combines the therapeutic art of colouring with the craft of creative writing, and provides you with all the prompts needed to help turn your initial light bulb moment into something special.